# A GOOD-NIGHT KISS

Caroline unlocked the door, stepped into the foyer, and turned to face him. "I don't think I have to tell you that I had a wonderful time this evening."

"I'm glad," he murmured, taking her into his arms. "But the evening's not quite over yet."

Caroline's arms encircled his neck. "No?"

"No," he replied, just before his lips captured hers. Unlike their previous kiss, there was no hesitation. His mouth moved slowly over hers. His hands stroked her back, coming to rest on the curves of her hips.

Caroline's fingers caressed the nape of his neck. The smell of his cologne mingled with his own scent as he pulled her closer. Engulfed in an aura of desire, she discarded her resolve to be sure of the depth of his feelings before becoming intimately involved.

# BOOK YOUR PLACE ON OUR WEBSITE AND MAKE THE ARABESQUE ROMANCE CONNECTION!

We've created a customized website just for our very special Arabesque readers, where you can get the inside scoop on everything that's going on with Arabesque romance novels.

When you come online, you'll have the exciting opportunity to:

- View covers of upcoming books

- Learn about our future publishing schedule (listed by publication month and author)

- Find out when your favorite authors will be visiting a city near you

- Search for and order backlist books

- Check out author bios and background information

- Send e-mail to your favorite authors

- Join us in weekly chats with authors, readers and other guests

- Get writing guidelines

- AND MUCH MORE!

Visit our website at
http://www.arabesquebooks.com

# EVERYTHING TO GAIN

## Marilyn Tyner

ARABESQUE

BOOKS

**BET Publications, LLC**
www.bet.com
www.arabesquebooks.com

ARABESQUE BOOKS are published by

BET Publications, LLC
c/o BET BOOKS
One BET Plaza
1900 W Place NE
Washington, D.C. 20018-1211

All Kensington Titles, Imprints and Distributed Lines are available at special quantity discounts for bulk purchases for sales
promotions, premiums, fund-raising, and educational or institu-
tional use. Special book excerpts or customized printings can
also be created to fit specific needs. For details, write or phone
the office of the Kensington special sales manager: Kensington
Publishing Corp., 850 Third Avenue, New York, NY 10022,
attn: Special Sales Department, Phone: 1-800-221-2647.

First Printing: March 2001

10  9  8  7  6  5  4  3  2  1
Printed in the United States of America

## ACKNOWLEDGMENTS

My thanks to Ann Harris, Assistant District Attorney of Cobb County in Georgia, for general information concerning possible sentences for some crimes. My thanks also to Debra Wierzbowski, my attorney's secretary, who referred me to Ms. Harris.

Other than these two people, I believe I have previously acknowledged each person to whom I owe a specific amount of gratitude. But I would like to also thank my family, friends, and acquaintances who have given me moral support and encouragement in my efforts. A special thanks goes to my readers, especially those of you who have written or e-mailed to let me know how much you enjoy my novels.

# Chapter One

Derek paused briefly outside of his brother's private office. "Is he alone, Karla?"

Ian's secretary nodded. "Yes, but he's on the telephone."

Derek pushed open the door and entered just as Ian hung up the telephone. "Hey Derek. How's the job going?"

"So far, so good," he said, taking a seat on the opposite side of the desk. "Everything seems to be running smoothly. I'm ready to install the new security system."

"I have the feeling this may only be the beginning of this problem. I don't suppose you've had any luck tracing the hacker?"

Derek shook his head. "Not yet. Maybe I'll have better luck before I'm finished. The new system might help to make it a little easier."

"Well, our main concern right now is restoring the nine-one-one system. All we can do is hope it will help prevent the same problem in the future."

Derek sighed. "The problem is that there may be more than one hacker and even if we catch one of them, there'll be others working just as hard to get into the system. It might be only a matter of time before one of them finds his way past the new security measures."

Ian nodded. "We'd only be kidding ourselves if we didn't acknowledge that possibility. We know, and our clients know, that this system may not be a permanent safeguard."

Ian rose from his chair and walked over to the credenza that extended along the wall to his left. "Can I get you anything to drink?"

"No, thanks."

Ian poured a glass of orange juice for himself and rejoined his brother. Taking his seat once again, he picked up a slip of paper from the desk and looked at his brother.

"How much longer do you think you'll need to finish the job?"

"Maybe a week. Why?"

"I've had two more calls for us to install security systems. One was from an investment company in Chicago. The other is from a large insurance company in Hartford. I told them we wouldn't be able to start until after the holidays since neither job involves any real urgency. If you have no objection, I'll take the job in Chicago. I don't think it will take as long as the insurance company job."

Derek shrugged. "That's fine with me."

Ian handed the slip of paper to his brother. "That's the name and telephone number of your contact person."

"I'll give him a call in a few days. By then I should have a better idea of when I'll finish this job." Derek rose from the chair. "By the way, have you finished your Christmas shopping?"

"No, I'll probably be out there on Christmas Eve, as usual."

Derek smiled. "For someone who's usually so organized, it amazes me that you're always so disorganized when it comes to Christmas shopping."

"That's because I believe in taking my time to find exactly the right gift."

His brother laughed outright at that statement. "I guess that's as good an excuse as any." He started toward the door. "I'll see you for Christmas dinner."

*Connecticut*

After spending Christmas with her parents, Caroline returned home the day before New Year's Eve. The holiday had been the usual mixture of the peace and calm of the Christmas Eve church service and the bedlam of Christmas day. Her siblings and their families, including seven children under the age of ten, had descended on her parents' house by lunchtime.

She always enjoyed sharing the holiday with her family. She hated admitting that in the past few years, there had been moments when the experience made her feel a void in her own life.

Whenever she watched her siblings and their spouses together, she felt a pang of longing. Even her parents, after almost forty years of marriage, were obviously deeply in love with each other. She supposed that was what she was looking for with Malcolm.

She and Malcolm had made tentative plans to attend a friend's party on New Year's Eve. When she arrived at home, there was a message from him saying that he had decided to remain in Virginia until after New Year's Day. She was not surprised and, strangely, not very disappointed.

Caroline did not hear from Malcolm until two days after she had returned to school. He called with an invitation to dinner, but no apology for missing the New Year's Eve party or excuse for not even calling to wish her a happy New Year. Against her better judgment, Caroline accepted his invitation. That date led to another and another. During the next few weeks they fell into their previous routine of dating.

Their usual routine was broken when he invited her to dinner at an expensive restaurant in one of the local hotels early in February. Their dates usually consisted of dinner at modest restaurants and sometimes a movie.

Dinner proceeded much as usual until the meal ended and they were having their coffee. "I have a surprise for you. It's also somewhat of an apology for missing the New Year's Eve party," Malcolm said, sliding an envelope across the table.

"Open it," he urged, when she hesitated.

Caroline thought it was rather late for an apology, but she did as he instructed. Inside the envelope was an itinerary for a weekend at a ski resort. "What's this?"

"Just what it looks like. It's a reservation for a romantic Valentine's Day weekend, skiing optional."

Caroline looked again at the papers in her hand. "Where's mine? This is just a reservation for one."

"It's a reservation for one room, two people."

Caroline took a deep breath and looked more closely at the paper in her hand. "You made these arrangements without consulting me? And you have the nerve to call it an apology?"

Malcolm reached over and took her hand in his. He smiled. "Come on, baby, don't you think it's time? You know how I feel about you. I don't understand why you're making this into such a big deal."

Caroline took another deep breath and pulled her hand from his grasp. ''I guess that's the difference in the way we think, Malcolm,'' she said, taking her napkin from her lap and placing it on the table. ''As far as I'm concerned, physical intimacy is a big deal. It's clear to me that the relationship we have isn't enough for you and I'm not prepared to take the next step.''

''Are you saying what I think you're saying?''

''I'm saying I think it's time for us to forget it.''

''Just like that?''

She shook her head. ''No, Malcolm, not just like that. It's been coming for a while. I'd suggest that we give ourselves a break from each other, but I don't think that would make any difference.''

She stood up. ''Good-bye, Malcolm.''

Before he could utter another word, she walked away from the table. She was quite calm and more upset with herself than she was with him. She finally admitted that what she was seeking was not going to be found with Malcolm.

Malcolm made no attempt to go after her. He picked up the envelope she had dropped on the table and shrugged.

Why had she let this go on so long? Her only excuse was that she had thought that at least they were good friends. She had told herself that their friendship might grow into something more. She had held onto the relationship hoping to feel some special spark to indicate that ''something more.'' This latest development made her wonder if the friendship itself had been real or only a game to get her into bed.

Caroline was unaware that their exchange had caught the attention of another customer leaving the restaurant. Derek had not heard the words, but her attitude and abrupt departure indicated more than a minor disagreement. That and his shock when he recognized her prompted him to follow her to the lobby.

Memories of Caroline had crossed his mind while he had prepared for this trip. Her family had lived in New Haven when she attended college in Atlanta, but he had never considered the possibility of running into her after all these years. After they broke up, he had heard nothing more about her. He never knew if she had returned to Connecticut or moved on to some other state after graduation.

Caroline approached the hotel desk. "Would you call a taxi for me, please?"

"Sure, miss."

He took her name and dialed the number. A moment later, the clerk hung up the telephone. "I'm afraid they're saying it will be a while before they can send someone."

"How long?"

"At least an hour."

Caroline shrugged. "I don't have much choice. Thank you."

"Maybe I can help," came a voice from behind. Her mind had no time to register the familiarity of the rich baritone voice.

When she turned to face her would-be rescuer, Caroline was confronted by the same man who had watched her leave the restaurant a few minutes earlier. Her eyes widened. Her heartbeat quickened and her mouth went dry. Derek Roberts was the last person she would have expected to meet in a Hartford hotel.

Derek repeated his offer. "Maybe I can help."

Caroline had difficulty forming a coherent thought. "Help?"

He gestured toward the desk clerk. "I heard what he said about the taxi. Can I give you a lift?"

"What . . . what are you doing here?"

"I'm in town on business. I caught a glimpse of you as you were leaving the restaurant. I could hardly believe my eyes. I had to follow you to make sure it was really you."

"You're staying here at the hotel?"

Derek nodded. Now that they were face to face, it was impossible for him to simply walk away. He repeated his offer. "Can I give you a lift?"

Caroline shook her head. She was not prepared for a tête-à-tête with this man from her past. "I don't want to inconvenience you. I live outside of Hartford, in New Britain."

"That's not far, is it?"

"No, it's not far."

"I have no other plans for this evening." He instructed the clerk to cancel the taxi. Then he took her coat from her arms. "Shall we go?"

Caroline could think of no graceful way to refuse his offer. He helped her on with her coat, his fingers brushing the nape of her neck as he adjusted the collar. She took a deep breath in an attempt to stifle the slight shiver that traveled down her spine. Taking her by the elbow, he urged her toward the elevator to the parking garage.

After they were settled in the car, he turned to face her. "What's the best route?"

The walk to the car had given her the opportunity to regain her composure. "Do you know how to get to I-84?"

"That much I can do."

A few minutes later, they were on their way. During the first part of the drive they were both silent, avoiding any mention of the past. Derek opened the conversation and they talked briefly about their respective careers. When they turned off the main highway, he changed the subject.

"You seemed upset at the hotel, even before you learned that the taxi would be delayed. What was that all about?"

Caroline considered telling him it was none of his business. Instead, keeping her gaze on the road, she replied, "Nothing much, just putting an end to a relationship."

Derek frowned. "You seem to be quite good at ending relationships."

Caroline abruptly glanced at him. "What does that mean?"

"I think it's self-explanatory."

Caroline grabbed the door handle. "Stop the car. You can let me out here," she demanded.

They were on a nearly deserted stretch of road. Derek's gaze never left the road.

"I don't think so. I'm not letting you out of the car this late at night in the middle of nowhere."

"I'll be fine."

Derek sighed. "Caroline, we can either drive around all night or you can finish giving me the directions to your house. It's your choice, but I'm not stopping the car out here."

The fact that he had not apologized for his remark did not escape Caroline. From what she remembered of his personality, she had no reason to believe he was bluffing about driving around all night if necessary. She gave him the directions he had requested.

When he pulled into the driveway of her town house, Caroline did not wait for him to open the car door; she got out without a word. Derek followed her up the walkway and waited patiently until she was safely inside.

He then returned to his car and turned the key in the ignition, but he did not drive away immediately. He sat there for a few minutes, watching as the lights in the house shifted from the first floor to a dim glow on the upper level.

She had changed little in the years since he had last seen her. The first evidence of that had come when he followed her from the restaurant. The form-fitting dress enhanced the tempting curves he remembered so well. Closer contact revealed the reddish-bronze complexion that was as smooth and clear as it had been when she was barely out of her teens. In fact, she still looked young enough to pass for a high school student.

Her hair was longer than he remembered. When he had met her years earlier, she wore it short and curly. Her current shoulder-length, smoother style suited her well, drawing attention to her eyes. He remembered her expressive eyes, how their color could change from being as soft and inviting as rich dark chocolate or, when she was angry, as black and hard as a lump of coal.

He had heard somewhere that a person's eyes were the mirror of the soul. He questioned the truth of that. If that had indeed been the case, he should have had some warning of her deceitfulness.

Derek glanced at the house again. It now sat in total darkness and he realized he had been sitting in his car for quite some time. He shook his head to clear it of disturbing memories and backed out of the driveway.

# Chapter Two

The next morning Caroline awakened and dragged herself out of bed. She had slept fitfully the previous night, her subconscious filled with thoughts of Derek. She might have handled the unexpected meeting more easily if it had not stirred up feelings she thought were long dead.

It had been six years since she had seen or spoken to him. He had said he was in Hartford on business. That would explain why he was alone. In their brief conversation the previous evening, she had deliberately avoided asking him any questions about a wife or children.

Her mind drifted back to the moment when she had first learned that he was engaged. She had managed to maintain her composure when she was confronted by his angry fiancée. It was when she was alone that she had allowed herself to fall apart. For months, she had wondered if she would ever recover from the pain. It had been difficult, but eventually the pain had eased and she thought she had put him completely out of her mind.

His comment about her ability to end relationships had taken her by surprise. He had been engaged to another woman the entire time he was dating her. What had he expected her to do when she found out?

The rest of the day and the following week, Caroline carried on with her usual activities, but thoughts of Derek were always in the back of her mind. She had a message from Malcolm when she arrived home on Thursday, suggesting they discuss their relationship. She erased the message with no intention of returning his call. As far as she was concerned, there was nothing more to discuss.

Aside from her previous doubts that their relationship had a future, she now had to consider the fact that she was still attracted to Derek. In spite of the hurt he had inflicted years earlier and the anger he had aroused when he drove her home, the feelings she had had for him were still very much alive.

That discovery gave her pause for further reflection when she received a telephone call from her former college roommate. The two had kept in touch after graduation and, for years, Vanessa had urged her to come for a visit. Caroline had finally agreed and planned to drive to Atlanta during her summer break.

"I hope you haven't changed your mind about coming here this summer."

"No, Vanessa, I haven't changed my mind," she assured her.

She had been looking forward to the visit until her recent encounter with Derek. In their brief meeting, she had learned that he still lived in Atlanta. She knew how much this visit meant to Vanessa and she could not bring herself to disappoint her friend. If she backed out now, she would have to come up with a good excuse. After some consideration, she decided that she was being ridiculous to even think about cancelling her trip. Atlanta was a big city.

"Actually, I called to see if you'd be interested in spending the entire summer here. I don't know if you remember Angela Wilson. She was a couple of years ahead of us in school."

"I remember her. She was a teaching assistant in one of our classes, wasn't she?"

"That's right. Anyway, she's the director of a community center in Decatur that has an after-school and summer tutoring program. One of the summer program volunteers wants to take this summer off to spend more time with her children, but she doesn't want to leave Angela shorthanded. Is there any chance I could talk you into filling in for her?"

"I don't know, Vanessa. Is it an all-day program?"

"Oh no, just a few hours in the afternoon."

"Well, let me think about it. I'll let you know in a couple of weeks."

The two women talked for a while longer. Caroline considered telling Vanessa about her encounter with Derek, but she was afraid she might reveal too much of her feelings. Vanessa knew about their relationship years earlier. If she guessed that Caroline was still attracted to Derek, it would undoubtedly lead to a discussion Caroline wanted to avoid.

Two weeks later, Caroline called Vanessa with her decision. She had no special plans for the summer and had already turned down the opportunity to teach summer school.

"I've decided since I have nothing better to do with my summer, I might as well spend it helping Angela."

"Are you still planning to drive down?"

''That's the plan. It's probably an even better idea since I'll need a car if I'm going to volunteer at the center.''

''As far as that's concerned, Angela could probably arrange transportation with one of the other workers at the center. If you need a car for other purposes, you could borrow mine or rent one for a day or two at a time. I'm not sure it's a good idea for you to drive that distance alone.''

''I'll be careful, Vanessa. I'll stop each evening before dark.''

''Well, if you insist. Give me a call before you leave.''

''I will.''

After hanging up from her conversation with Vanessa, Caroline dialed her parents' number.

When her mother answered, she explained ''I wasn't sure I told you I'll be going to Jason's for Easter, so I thought I'd better give you a call,'' Caroline said.

''No, you hadn't told me, but Jason mentioned it the last time I spoke with him.''

''I can't wait to see Justin. I talked to Leah a few weeks ago and she said he's talking now. I mean really talking, not the usual babbling.''

''I know. I could hear him in the background when Jason called the other day. Of course, as soon as Jason put the telephone to his ear, he clammed up. After 'Hi, Grandma,' he wouldn't say another word.''

They talked for a while, Grace filling Caroline in on her other siblings. ''How's Malcolm?'' she asked before hanging up.

''As far as I know, he's fine. We're not seeing each other anymore. We broke up a few weeks ago.''

That statement came as no surprise to Grace. She had expected it was only a matter of time before their relationship ended. Her daughter had never talked much about Malcolm, and the few times she mentioned him, she showed little emotion or enthusiasm. That suited Grace fine. She had only met the young man once, and had not been greatly impressed.

"Are you all right?" Grace asked.

"I'm fine, Mom. It's not like it was a big surprise. I've seen it coming for a while."

"Don't let it bother you, honey. He just wasn't the right man for you. Have a good trip. Kiss everyone for me."

"I will. I'll talk to you when I get back."

Caroline hung up the telephone and thought about her mother's words. She was beginning to wonder if there *was* a right man for her. She thought she had met the right man years ago, and that belief had only ended up causing her a lot of pain.

When Caroline's plane landed in Pittsburgh, she was greeted at the gate by her brother and sister-in-law. Thanks to her nephew Justin's shrieks of delight as he watched the airplanes taking off and landing, they were easy to spot in the crowd.

"How was the flight?" Leah asked as Jason urged his son away from the window.

"Fine."

Jason handed Justin to his mother and took Caroline's bags. "Is this it?"

"That's it. I didn't want to wait around in the baggage area so I managed to pack light for a change."

Caroline's and Leah's almost constant chatter on the drive from the airport made the trip seem to pass in no time. When they arrived at the house, Jason retrieved Caroline's bag from the back of the van while Leah lifted a sleeping Justin from his car seat.

"I'll take him up to bed, honey," Jason insisted.

"I can carry my bag, Jason," Caroline offered.

"No problem," her brother said. He took his son in one arm, her bag in the other, and entered the house.

Caroline and Leah followed. "Are you hungry?" Leah asked.

Caroline shook her head. "No, thanks, I had a big breakfast at the airport while I was waiting for my flight."

"How about some coffee or tea?"

"Tea sounds fine."

A few minutes later they were joined by Jason. The three sat at the table and chatted for a while before Caroline suggested she should go upstairs and unpack.

"I'll show you the way," Leah insisted.

Leah sat on the side of the bed chatting as Caroline unpacked. She had almost finished when Justin made it known that he was awake and ready to be freed from his crib.

"I'll be back in a few minutes," Leah said. "He hasn't quite mastered the job of getting out of the crib, but I caught him trying a few times."

She returned as promised with Justin in tow, and offered to give Leah a tour of the house. Jason, an architect, had designed it himself and they had moved in the previous summer.

"I went a little crazy at first trying to finish the decorating, but I didn't want to hire a professional. You wouldn't believe how much time I've spent watching decorating shows on television and reading magazines. You can really get some great ideas from them."

She led her to Justin's room first. "I had a lot of fun with this one. I wanted to do something that would grow with him. You saw how fascinated he is with airplanes. I decided that was the way to go."

Caroline smiled as she looked around the room. Not only had Leah found a wallpaper border with airplanes, but a lamp made from a toy airplane and even a child-sized airplane that Justin could ride. The most fascinating touches were the small plastic airplanes and fluffy clouds suspended from the ceiling.

"It's great, Leah. You really put a lot of work into this."

"Thanks. I have to give Jason his due. He helped with the clouds and planes hanging from the ceiling. Your father made the little plane for Justin to ride. His woodworking skills are amazing, considering it's only a hobby."

They left the child's room and continued the tour. The master bedroom and guest room had been completed, but the other two bedrooms were empty.

"Jason convinced me that there was no rush to decorate all of the rooms, so I concentrated on the living area. I'm still working on the family room and dining room."

"Well, you've done a wonderful job, to have been in the house less than a year." Caroline smiled. "Besides, you may need those other bedrooms for children."

During dinner that evening, Jason mentioned her summer plans. "I talked to Mom a few days ago. She said you're planning to go to Atlanta this summer. You're driving down?"

Caroline sighed. Her brother had always been overprotective of her. "Yes, Jason, I'm going to Atlanta and I'm planning to drive. I've already had this discussion with Mom and Dad and Vanessa. I promise to be careful. I won't be taking any side roads and I won't be driving at night. I also promised Mom I'd call every night when I stop for the day."

Jason held up his hands in surrender. "Okay, okay, I get the message. How long are you staying in Atlanta?"

"As a matter of fact, I'll be spending the entire summer there." She told them about Vanessa's request.

"How does Malcolm feel about your being away all summer?" Jason asked.

Leah rolled her eyes.

"Malcolm and I are no longer dating," Caroline replied, focusing her attention on her plate.

Jason and Leah exchanged glances. Caroline's tone of voice said more than her words. She seemed more resigned than unhappy. Leah immediately changed the subject, asking what her volunteer work would involve.

When that topic had been exhausted, Jason attempted to make up for his earlier faux pas by telling her about his latest project. There was no further mention of Malcolm during Caroline's visit.

# Chapter Three

*Atlanta*

"Come on, Uncle Derek, help me," Savannah urged, pulling Derek's hand.

Derek smiled at the child's pleading.

"I thought the idea was for you to find them yourself. Wouldn't it be cheating if I helped you?"

Savannah frowned. "I'm only a little girl. All the other kids are bigger than me. Please, help me find just one, or maybe two."

He stifled a chuckle and shook his head. His niece could be a real manipulator sometimes. It was good that her parents saw through her questionable propositions. She never succeeded with them, which was why she saved most of her efforts for her uncle or her grandparents.

"Uh-huh, or three or four or five. I'll make a deal with you. If you really try hard and don't find any eggs before the time is up, I'll think about giving you some hints. But you have to try on your own first.''

Savannah continued to frown, shuffling her feet in the grass and trying very hard to look pathetic. Derek covered his mouth to hide his smile.

''You're wasting time, Savannah.''

''Okay, but you promise you'll help if I can't find any, right?''

Derek nodded. Savannah was not totally satisfied, but she was aware that she had lost the battle. She skipped off in search of hidden Easter eggs. Derek watched her, his smile fading as his mind traveled back six years.

''I see my daughter is up to her usual shenanigans,'' Ian said, breaking into what was beginning to be an unpleasant reverie for Derek.

''You can't really blame her for trying. I don't think she gets away with much, though.''

''Fortunately, that's true.''

Ian watched Savannah scramble around on the lawn. Her cries of joy a few minutes later told him she had been successful in her hunt. He had had no doubt that she could hold her own in the egg hunt, but she knew she had a better chance of winning if she could con an adult into helping her. He turned his attention back to his brother.

''We haven't had much chance to talk since you came back from Hartford. Since you haven't said anything to the contrary, I guess the installation of the security system went smoothly.''

Derek nodded. ''Sure, no problem. In fact, you may be getting some more calls. The director of operations seemed impressed with the system when I pointed out some of the features. Of course, time will tell how well it's working.''

''It held up well under our own testing. We'll just have to wait and see.''

* * *

Later that evening, as he drove home, Derek's thoughts returned to his young niece. He could not help thinking about his own hopes that had been dashed years ago. He had never spoken of them, had not even realized he had such hopes until they were destroyed.

He thought he had put the anger and disappointment of his loss behind him. Seeing Caroline again after all these years had resurrected those memories. That meeting had resurrected more than memories. It had rekindled the feelings he thought he had buried years ago.

He could have dealt with the anger and disappointment; it was the other feelings that were the real problem. How could he still be attracted to her, care for her, after what she did? The physical attraction could be easily explained. She was an attractive woman. What he felt was much more than a simple physical attraction.

The fact that Caroline was a thousand miles away should help him push those feelings aside. Even if his job required him to return to Connecticut, it was unlikely he would run into her again. In fact, he would make sure to do everything in his power to avoid that possibility.

*Connecticut*

Caroline finished packing the last of the boxes to be loaded into her car. She hated having to cart everything home and bring it back again in September, but she had learned her lesson about leaving personal classroom aids in the room during summer vacation.

She started toward the classroom door with the first of the boxes as the school custodian entered the room. "Need some help with those, Miss Duval?"

"I'd appreciate it, Mr. Michaels."

"Why don't you pull your car up to the side door? I'll start carrying these out."

Within fifteen minutes, the car was loaded. "Thanks, Mr. Michaels. Have a good summer."

"The same to you, Ms. Duval."

As he started toward the building, Caroline heard her name being called. She turned to greet a fellow teacher.

"Hi, Julie. What's up?"

"I just wanted to wish you a restful summer," her coworker said, smiling.

"The same to you. I don't know how restful it will be for you, though, with three kids at home."

"Well, I'll get a break next month. They'll be spending a few weeks with my parents. What about you? Any special plans?"

"As a matter of fact, I'll be helping a friend of a friend with her tutoring program."

"Talk about a busman's holiday. You haven't had enough of teaching during the school year?"

"It won't be so bad. It's only for a few hours a day and it'll be a change of scenery: Atlanta. In fact, I'm leaving tomorrow."

"I'd better let you go, then. Have a safe trip."

The women hugged. Caroline closed the trunk and waved to her friend as she proceeded to her own car. A few minutes later, she pulled out of the parking lot.


After unloading her school materials, Caroline donned more comfortable clothes. Then she sat down to eat the sandwich and salad that she had picked up on her way home.

She had mapped out her itinerary, planning overnight stops along the way. She estimated she would be able to reach Virginia by the end of the first day. If the weather remained clear, she could be in Atlanta by Friday afternoon.

After she packed, she called Vanessa. "I'm all packed and ready to go. I'll be leaving tomorrow. I expect to be in Atlanta by Friday, but I'll call if it looks like I'll be delayed beyond that."

"I'd better give you my number at work. If you get into town before five o'clock, call me." Vanessa gave her the number as well as directions to her house before she hung up a few minutes later.

Early the next morning Caroline loaded her suitcases into her car and made a last check of the house before calling her mother. "I just wanted to touch base with you. I'm all packed and I'll be leaving in a few minutes."

"Okay, baby, you drive carefully."

"I will. I'll call you this evening."


Caroline's trip went much as planned. She stopped earlier than she had planned on the third day when she encountered heavy rain. She arrived in Atlanta in the early evening on Friday. After stopping for gas, she looked at the directions Vanessa had given her. She thought they looked easy enough until she drove around for a while and realized she must have missed a turn.

She pulled into a Burger King parking lot, took her cell phone from the glove compartment, and dialed Vanessa's number.

"Caroline! I've been waiting for you. Where are you?"

"I'm lost."

She gave Vanessa her location and wrote down the new directions. A few minutes later, she pulled out of the parking lot and headed in the opposite direction from which she had been traveling. Half an hour later, she pulled into her friend's driveway.

Before Caroline rang the bell, Vanessa opened the door and threw her arms around her. "It's so good to see you again. Did you have any trouble with the new directions?"

"Not at all. I saw what I did wrong the first time. I missed the street sign for the turnoff. Once I found the right street, it was easy."

"Come on, I'll help you with your bags," Vanessa offered.

They returned to the house a few minutes later. "I'll show you to your room now. Did you eat dinner?"

"No, I was so close that I didn't want to stop."

"What with the delay of getting lost, you must be starved by now. I've been nibbling on the chicken salad I made, so I'm not very hungry. Do you want to unpack first?"

"Just let me take the clothes from the garment bag and hang them up. The rest can wait."

A short time later they were seated at the kitchen table, catching up on the events since they had last seen each other at Vanessa's wedding. Afterward, Vanessa kept her company while she unpacked. Then she gave her a tour of the house before they settled in Vanessa's bedroom and talked until the wee hours of the morning.

Caroline awoke late the next morning to the aroma of coffee. She made her way downstairs to the kitchen.

"Morning."

Vanessa turned to face her, a mug of coffee in her hand. "Good morning. Did you sleep okay?"

Caroline smiled. "The fact that it'll soon be lunchtime should answer that question."

"Do you want coffee?"

"Of course, but I can get it myself."

"I'll get it. You're a guest, for the first few days anyway. What would you like for breakfast?"

Caroline smiled. "You're really serious about this guest bit, aren't you?"

"Like I said, this is only for the first few days, so you'd better take advantage of it."

They continued the conversation over scrambled eggs and English muffins. "Do you have any plans for today?"

Vanessa shook her head. "I thought you might want to just relax today. That drive must have been tiring."

"It wasn't too bad. I had my CD's to keep me company and I stopped regularly to stretch my legs."

Caroline watched her friend as she loaded the dirty plates into the dishwasher. "So, how are you getting along, Vanessa, honestly?"

"Is that why you finally agreed to come for a visit—to make sure I wasn't pining away over my separation from Kevin?"

"No, that wasn't the reason, but I was concerned about you."

Vanessa sat back down and took a sip of coffee before answering. She shrugged. "It was hard at first. There are still times that I get a little down, but I'll get over it."

Caroline nodded. She looked down at her mug. There were questions on the tip of her tongue, but she hesitated to ask them. Vanessa had told her about the separation, but not much more than that.

"Caroline? What is it? You look like you're not sure I'm telling the truth."

"It's not that, Vanessa. I guess I'm just wondering what happened? You two were so much in love, even as far back as when we were in college."

There was no immediate reply from her friend. It occurred to Caroline that Vanessa might think she was prying.

"Hey, girlfriend, if you want to tell me it's none of my business, that's fine, as long as you understand that I'm not just asking out of curiosity."

Vanessa reached over and touched Caroline's hand. "I know that." She paused. "You asked me what happened. I don't know, except that we both were working long hours and he insisted on working almost every weekend. We never seemed to have time for each other.

"When I suggested we cut down on work and make more time for each other, he insisted that was impossible. It finally got to the point where I couldn't see any reason for staying together if we only saw each other for a few hours on the weekend."

"Do you still love him?"

Vanessa smiled weakly. "Of course, I still love him. You don't stop loving someone that easily."

"Do you think he still loves you?"

Vanessa sighed. "Sometimes I'm not so sure."

Caroline was hesitant to voice the possibility that had come to mind. "I have to ask: Do you think there's another woman, that he was having an affair?"

Her friend shook her head. "No, I don't have any reason to think that. And no, I'm not in denial. I considered that possibility. In fact, I called him at the office a few times when he said he was working late. He was always there and it appeared he was alone. There weren't any other clues to hint that it was anything more than work."

"Well, maybe he'll come to his senses and you two can work things out."

Vanessa shrugged again. "Maybe, but for now I'm getting my life in order with the assumption that that's not going to happen."

Later that afternoon, Caroline decided she had rested enough and she suggested they go out to dinner. Afterward, Vanessa gave her an abbreviated tour, pointing out some of the changes that had taken place in Atlanta since Caroline had moved back to Connecticut after graduation.

The day after Caroline's arrival, Vanessa called Angela and the three women met briefly at Angela's house before driving to the community center. Angela showed Caroline the classroom where she would be teaching.

"I really appreciate your help, Caroline. I'm sure Zoe, one of the other volunteers, will appreciate it even more. I tried to talk her into taking the summer off, with or without a replacement. After all, it's not like it's a paying job. I'm just grateful for all the volunteer work that she's put in this past year. I can hardly blame her for wanting to take a break and spend the summer with her family."

"I don't mind helping out. I usually teach summer school anyway. This will be a change from my usual routine. You mentioned that you teach literacy classes for adults, as well as tutor the children. Will you need me for that?"

"No, there's another teacher that handles that class. I'd really feel guilty about asking you to give up your evenings, too."

"How soon do you want me to start?"

"As soon as you can."

"Monday?"

"That'll be great! I didn't want to push. I thought you might want to do some sightseeing or shopping before we put you to work."

Caroline shook her head. "I'll only be working a few hours in the afternoons. That should leave me plenty of time for other activities."

Angela nodded. "It'll be good to have you here for a few days before Zoe takes her leave. We ask to see the students' report cards to give us an idea of their individual weaknesses. That way we can develop smaller groups within the classes. Zoe can probably help you with that planning.

"We've found that the most help is usually needed in science and math for the older age groups. We have two other teachers that work with those students. I think you'll find that you need to concentrate on reading and math skills for the younger children."

Angela gave Caroline a tour of the rest of the center as she explained more about the other programs they offered. "We were lucky to get this building. The location is great since it means that a lot of the students are within walking distance. For the others, it's easily accessed by public transportation."

She shrugged. "It's not the safest neighborhood in town, but we haven't had any problems. We have an alarm system that links directly to the police, and having the fenced-in parking area is a real plus. By the way, I'll get you a key to the gate by Monday."

When they finished at the center, Angela parted company with the other two women. Vanessa suggested another tour of Atlanta.

"Angela mentioned shopping and I feel obligated to take you to Lenox Square," Vanessa said, taking Caroline by the arm.

# Chapter Four

The following Monday, Caroline arrived at the center shortly after noon. She parked at the curb and went to get the key to the parking area.

Angela was nowhere in sight. She approached the reception desk. "Hi, I'm Caroline Duval. Is Angela around?"

"Hi, I'm Rita. Angela's on the phone. She left a key for you. It's for the empty lot on the side of the building."

Caroline nodded. "She showed me how to get in the gate when we stopped by on Saturday."

A short time later, Caroline reentered the building and was met by Angela.

"Hi, Caroline. Rita told me you were here. Did you have any trouble with the directions?"

"Not at all," Caroline assured her, shaking her head.

"Good, Zoe should be here shortly." The words had barely left her mouth when Zoe walked in the door.

"Hi, Zoe. Come and meet your replacement." She introduced the two women.

"It's really generous of you to give up your summer vacation to help us out," Zoe said as they shook hands.

"From what I've heard, you're the one who's been generous with her time."

Zoe shook her head. "I haven't done that much. The truth is, I was glad to be teaching again."

A few minutes later the two women adjourned to their classroom to prepare for the students, who would begin arriving at one o'clock. In addition to the other adult volunteer teachers, Angela had enlisted the aid of several teenagers to help with the elementary school students.

The afternoon passed quickly. Caroline was surprised when Zoe suggested it was time to wrap up for the day.

The rest of the week was much the same as Monday. As she worked with the children, Caroline felt a new appreciation for her choice of professions. She enjoyed her teaching job in Connecticut, but working with children who had all the advantages of a middle-class environment was very different from her volunteer situation.

"You're free for the rest of the summer. Enjoy." Caroline said to Zoe as they prepared to leave on Friday.

"Speaking of summer, I wanted to invite you and your friend to a barbecue on the Fourth of July. Angela's planning to come, and some of the other employees here."

"Thanks, Zoe, but I don't know if Vanessa's made other plans for us for the holiday."

"If not, bring her along. I owe her too, since she's the one who talked you into replacing me."

Caroline broached the subject with Vanessa that evening. "I don't really have any other plans," Vanessa said.

"You don't sound very enthusiastic about it."

Vanessa shrugged.

"I think it will do you good, Vanessa. Something tells me you haven't been out much in the past six months."

"I'll think about it. If I decide not to go, I hope it won't keep you from going."

"No, I won't let that keep me from going, but I intend to keep after you until you agree to come with me."

Vanessa rolled her eyes. "Then I guess I might as well agree and save myself some aggravation."

Caroline smiled. "Good, that's settled then."


On the following Tuesday, Caroline had reason to regret urging Vanessa to go to Zoe's barbecue. The last child had left the classroom when Angela poked her head in the door.

"Hi, I came to introduce you to another of our generous volunteers."

She entered the room, followed by the man who had haunted Caroline's thoughts for months. "Derek, this is Caroline Duval. She's agreed to take Zoe's place for the summer."

She turned to Caroline. Until that moment, Angela had not noticed the stricken look on Caroline's face. She was puzzled, but continued with the introductions.

"Derek is Zoe's brother-in-law. He periodically conducts a computer workshop in the evenings. He and his brother, Ian, have contributed a great deal to the success of this center."

Derek was the first of the two to speak. "We've met."

His tone of voice drew Angela's attention back to him. The look on his face was not as odd as Caroline's pained expression, but it was definitely not friendly.

"I'd better get set up," he said shortly. Then he was gone.

"Caroline? Are you all right?"

Caroline swallowed hard. "I'm fine," she insisted. "Just a little surprised."

Turning her attention to the pile of papers on her desk, she added, "I'll take these papers with me. I want to take my time to go over them."

Caroline gave no explanation for her reaction, nor for Derek's statement that they had met before. It was hard to believe that her reaction was just the result of meeting an old acquaintance, but Angela refrained from asking any questions.

"Well, I'll see you tomorrow," Angela replied, before retreating from the classroom.

After Angela left, Caroline plopped down in her chair. She took a deep breath. "I guess Atlanta's not as big as I'd hoped," she murmured to herself.

She finished gathering the papers and slipped them into her totebag. She wondered how often Derek came to the center. Not that it mattered. He seemed as eager as she was to avoid any further contact between them.

It was not until she was in her car that she recalled an important piece of information she had received from Angela. She was so shocked at seeing Derek that it had not registered when they were introduced. Derek was Zoe's brother-in-law.

When she had heard Zoe's last name, it had never occurred to her that she was related to Derek. "Roberts" was a fairly common last name.

With such a close connection, she could count on Derek being at the Fourth of July barbecue. She had already accepted Zoe's invitation. How could she back down now? What possible excuse could she give her?

The more she considered staying away from the barbecue, the more foolish she felt. Avoiding Derek would accomplish nothing. It was time she learned to cope with the fact that he was married to another woman.

She thought she had done that long ago. The fact that she had been unable to get him out of her mind in the last few months proved that her efforts had been unsuccessful.

She would attend the barbecue. She would attend and she would enjoy herself, and she would be pleasant to him and his wife.

Shortly after leaving Caroline's classroom, Derek prepared for the students' arrival, which was a little more than an hour away. As he set about arranging the papers for the practice exercise, part of his mind was elsewhere.

He had been complacent about the fact that a thousand miles separated him from Caroline. Ian had told him that a friend of Angela's had convinced one of her friends to help at the center for the summer. The idea that Caroline was Zoe's replacement was so far-fetched, it would never have entered his mind as a possibility. Why would she come all the way to Atlanta to volunteer at a community center?

Her reason for coming to Atlanta was unimportant. He was determined that her presence would not interfere with his work at the center, nor his life outside of the center. She had made her position clear six years ago, when she ended their relationship.

While Derek and Caroline were resolving not to let their past relationship interfere with enjoying the party, Ian and Zoe were perusing their plans for the event. They sat side by side on the sofa in the family room, going over the guest list.

"By the way," Zoe said, "I invited Caroline to the barbecue."

"Caroline?"

"The teacher who volunteered to replace me at the center. Did I tell you she came all the way from Connecticut?"

"Just to volunteer at the center?"

Zoe rolled her eyes and shook her head. "No, of course not. According to Angela, she was planning to visit her former college roommate, who's a friend of Angela's."

"And Angela convinced her to volunteer for the summer?"

"Actually, the roommate, Vanessa, convinced her."

A memory clicked in the back of Ian's mind. "You said she's from Connecticut?"

"That's right. Why?"

Ian hesitated, biting his lip. He shook his head as if to clarify the vague memories of the sparse information he had received from his brother years ago.

"Nothing, really. Derek dated a girl from Connecticut when he was a teaching assistant and working on his master's degree. I'm almost sure her name was Caroline. It's probably just a coincidence."

"I don't understand. What's the big deal? Even if it is the same woman Derek dated, that was years ago." She looked closely at her husband. "Or was there more involved than just dating? The fact that you remember her name tells me that's a possibility."

"I'm not sure. Derek didn't confide much to anyone about the relationship, so I can't remember any details. But you're right, there was something in his attitude that made me believe she was different from the other women he had dated, especially whenever he mentioned her name. He seemed to be more serious about their relationship than any of the others. I got the impression that he was in love with her, even considering proposing marriage.''

''What happened?''

Ian shook his head. ''I don't know. All I know is, I asked him about her one day and he said they had broken up. His attitude made it clear that he didn't want to discuss it.''

''That was all? I mean, I wouldn't expect him to go into any details about their relationship, but it seems he'd tell you more than that. He didn't give you any idea of what went wrong?''

''Not in words, but there was a change in him for a long time afterward. That's the other reason I thought there was more than casual dating involved.''

''Well, if it is the same Caroline, I still think that after all these years they would have gotten over any differences they might have had.''

''Maybe.'' Ian pulled her close and kissed her cheek. ''Sometimes it's not that easy if you were in love.''


That evening at dinner, Caroline decided she should tell Vanessa about Derek. ''I badgered you into coming to the barbecue for your sake, but I think I may need you there for my mine.''

Vanessa sighed. ''I already agreed to go, Caroline. You don't have to come up with any more reasons to convince me.''

Caroline shook her head. ''I'm serious.''

Vanessa looked more closely at her friend. ''What happened?''

''Do you know who Zoe's husband is?'' she asked, pushing her food around on her plate.

"No, the subject never came up in my conversations with Angela."

"Her husband is Ian Roberts, Derek's brother."

It was Vanessa's turn to focus her attention on her food. She took a deep breath and said, "It's been six years, Caroline. Does it really matter after all this time?"

"It probably shouldn't, but it does." She told her friend about her encounter with Derek in Hartford.

Vanessa stared at her. "You actually ran into Derek in Connecticut? I can't believe it."

Caroline took her eyes off her food and met her friend's gaze. "You can't believe it? Imagine how I felt."

"Was Marquita with him?"

"No, Marquita wasn't with him. He said he was there on business."

"What did you talk about? Did he mention his family?"

"No, and I tried very hard to avoid that topic. There wasn't much conversation. We talked about our jobs mostly. I was just glad it was a short drive."

"A short drive? You went somewhere with him?"

Caroline told her about the problem with the taxi and Derek's insistence on driving her home. "I was so shocked I couldn't even come up with an excuse to refuse."

"Caroline, I have a feeling that there's a lot you're not telling me—and that's fine if you'd rather not talk about it."

"That's not it, Vanessa. There just isn't much to tell."

"You just admitted that seeing him again after all this time does matter. That, and avoiding any mention of his family, tells me you still feel something for him. What about him? How did he act?"

"He acted like he did the last time I talked to him." She made no mention of his comment that she seemed to have no trouble ending relationships.

"How was that? You never talked about it and I never asked. Since you haven't told me to mind my own business, I might as well ask it now. What exactly did he say when you broke up with him? What was his excuse for not telling you about Marquita?"

Caroline became engrossed in her food once again. She had never told her friend about the conversation that ended her relationship with Derek.

"Caroline? Is this where you tell me to mind my own business?"

Caroline's gaze stayed focused on her plate. "No. The truth is, I didn't tell him. I just told him I didn't think we should see each other anymore."

Vanessa's eyes widened. "You never told him why?"

"No, I didn't see any point in it. I assumed he'd put two and two together and guessed that I found out about his engagement. I wasn't in any mood to hear his excuses for what he'd done."

Vanessa nodded slowly. "I guess I can understand that. I remember how upset you were."

"It doesn't matter now. That's all past history. I'm just not looking forward to seeing him and Marquita hanging all over each other."

Vanessa asked no more questions. The subject was dropped as far as the conversation was concerned, but it was still in the back of her mind. She had seen Caroline and Derek together years ago and she had been convinced that they were deeply in love. But then, she had been convinced that she and Kevin also were deeply in love. *And look at us now,* she thought.

# Chapter Five

Caroline did not see Derek during the next two weeks, although he crossed her mind often during the day and his image flitted through her dreams at night. She had no control over the unconscious workings of her mind. Neither did she have any control over the likelihood of seeing him again in the flesh. It was almost a certainty that he would attend the barbecue at his brother's house.

On the day before the party, Caroline stopped by Angela's office before leaving the center. Since the day she introduced them, Angela's only comment concerning Derek had been to ask how Caroline had met him. Caroline told her that they had met while she was in college, but she had volunteered no other information. Angela had taken the hint.

Although Angela sometimes discussed what was happening in the other classes at the center, she had made no mention of Derek or his computer classes. Caroline was unsure if that omission was because Angela was aware of her discomfort or if she simply thought Caroline had no interest in the computer classes.

She poked her head in Angela's door. "I guess I'll see you tomorrow, if I don't get lost trying to find my way to Zoe's house."

Angela smiled. "It's not difficult. She did give you directions, didn't she?"

"Yes, she gave me her telephone number, too, just in case I have a problem."

"Good, Vanessa told me she's coming with you. She's never been to Zoe's, but at least she's familiar with the area so she might be able to help with the directions."

Caroline nodded, waved, and turned to go. "Okay, see you tomorrow."

The next day, Caroline stood in front of the closet in Vanessa's guest room, staring at the clothes she had brought with her. She finally settled on a pair of royal blue, crinkled-cotton shorts, a matching tunic top, and sandals. After pulling her hair back into a French braid, she took a deep breath and decided she was as ready as she would ever be.

She and Vanessa arrived at Ian and Zoe's house shortly after one o'clock. There were a number of cars already parked in the wide driveway. Caroline pulled into the space behind the last car.

The were greeted at the door by Zoe. "Hi, did you have any trouble finding the house?"

"Not at all. Your directions were great."

Zoe ushered them toward the back of the house. "Everyone's out back."

When they reached the deck at the rear of the house, Zoe pointed to a group of children running on the lawn beyond the deck. "The little whirlwind in the purple shorts is my daughter, Savannah. I just put Blake down for his nap."

Caroline and Vanessa followed her across the deck toward a man standing guard over the large double grill. "This is my husband, Ian."

As Zoe performed the introductions, Caroline could barely keep from staring. She had never met Derek's brother, but the family resemblance made the relationship unmistakable.

"What can I get you to drink?" Zoe asked. After filling their requests, she introduced them to the others assembled on the deck.

Angela arrived shortly after Zoe finished the introductions. Zoe returned to her duties as hostess and left them on their own to mingle with the other guests. After introducing Vanessa and Caroline to a few of her acquaintances, Angela led the way to one of the tables scattered on the the lower level of the large deck. The three of them settled down with their drinks. A few minutes later, their conversation was interrupted by a voice calling to Vanessa.

Vanessa looked in the direction of the deck. "Keisha!" she cried, jumping up from her chair and running across the lawn toward the newcomer.

A moment later, the two women were hugging and laughing. As they neared the table, Keisha recognized Caroline.

"Caroline? I thought you looked familiar when I saw you from over there. It's good to see you again. What brings you to Atlanta?"

"Vanessa's been badgering me for years. I finally agreed to come for a visit and then she decided that wasn't enough. I'm here for the summer, helping Angela with her tutoring program at the community center."

Vanessa interrupted, laying her hand on Angela's shoulder. "You remember Angela Wilson, don't you?"

"I'm not sure." She held out her hand. "It's nice to meet

you now, though.'' She turned her attention back to Caroline.
''So you're the teacher who's filling in for Zoe.''

''You know Zoe?''

''Well, actually, I only know Zoe through Ian. I work for
him as a computer analyst.''

Vanessa returned to her seat and Caroline was grateful
that Keisha's attention was turned to pulling up a chair from
one of the other tables. If Keisha worked for Ian, she knew
Derek. As far as Caroline knew, Keisha was unaware of the
extent of her involvement with Derek when they were in
college. She and Keisha had never been close friends, but
college grapevines being what they were, it was possible
she knew the whole story.

''We really should be ashamed of ourselves for not keeping in touch,'' Keisha said, shaking her head at Vanessa.
''Especially since we both live right here in Atlanta, or at
least close by.''

The conversation centered on the events of the two friends'
lives in the years since they had graduated from college.
Caroline relaxed and had almost forgotten her doubts about
accepting Zoe's invitation until Derek arrived a few minutes
later. She was surprised to see that he was alone, but she
refrained from commenting. Vanessa had no such qualms.

''Derek's wife didn't come with him?'' she asked Angela.

Angela's brows knit in confusion. She and Keisha spoke
at the same time. ''His wife?''

''Derek's not married,'' Angela added. ''What made you
think that?''

Vanessa tried to cover her surprise without giving away
any information about Caroline and Derek's past relationship. She shrugged and sipped her lemonade.

''I guess I'm just remembering something from years ago
that gave me the idea that he was married.''

Angela looked askance at her friend. She guessed that

there were details that Vanessa had deliberately omitted. She also guessed that her friend's reticence was connected to Caroline's strange reaction when she had introduced her to Derek.

She watched Caroline's reaction as Derek walked over to his brother. The two men exchanged a few words before Derek moved away. He mingled with the guests, slowly making his way toward their group. Caroline was unaware that she stiffened slightly as he got closer.

Caroline was one of the first people Derek had seen when he scanned the area and the guests assembled on the deck. Zoe had made no mention of inviting her, but he had had no doubt that she would be included on the list of guests. He would have preferred to ignore Caroline, but he could hardly avoid the courtesy of acknowledging Angela and Keisha. Forcing a smile to his lips, he approached the group.

"Hello, ladies," he murmured.

"Hi, Derek, it's nice to see you again," Angela said. She gestured to Vanessa and Caroline. "You know Caroline, but have you met Vanessa?"

"Yes, we've met."

His curt response alerted Angela. In an effort to avoid another awkward moment, she continued the conversation. She asked him about the new group of computer students and they talked for a few minutes before Derek insisted he had to go help to his brother man the grills.

Caroline watched Derek walk away and then forced her attention back to the group seated at the table. Once he was out of close proximity, she relaxed.

"I'm glad you're back," Ian said to Derek as he approached. "Would you keep an eye on these steaks while I see if Zoe needs some help in the kitchen?"

"Sure. Am I supposed to leave them rare or let them get well done?"

"Just make them all medium. That should be acceptable to everyone."

Later that afternoon, Caroline and Vanessa were alone at the table when Zoe approached with her son in her arms. "This is Blake. Say 'hello,' sweetheart," she prompted and the child hid his face in his mother's shoulder.

"He's adorable." Caroline said. "How old is he?"

"Nineteen months, but sometimes I think he's trying to get a jump on the 'terrible twos.' "

"I have a nephew who turned two a few months ago."

The women chatted for a while before Savannah claimed her mother's attention. She came limping toward them, her lip quivering as she tried hard not to cry.

"What happened, honey?" Zoe asked, setting Blake on his somewhat unsteady feet.

"Mark pushed me and I fell." She held out her knee. "See what he made me do?"

"You'll be all right. I don't think Mark meant to hurt you. You were both running." Zoe held out her hand to her daughter. "Come with me and I'll fix it."

"I'll keep Blake if he'll stay with me," Caroline offered, lifting the child onto her lap. She waited for him to protest, but he became fascinated with her earrings and was quite content to stay.

Zoe returned a few minutes later and sat down to chat. Another crisis overcome, Savannah ran off to join the other children.

Blake scrambled to get down from Caroline's lap. After she helped him down, he toddled over to his mother. A few minutes later, Ian approached and lifted his son in his arms.

"I'll keep him occupied," he said to Zoe, "and give you two a chance to talk."

Caroline smiled as he walked away with Blake waving good-bye. "He and Savannah must keep you busy. I can understand why you needed a break from your volunteer work at the center."

"It wasn't so bad during the school year. Savannah was in nursery school and I only tutored for a couple of hours in the after-school program. I decided that this summer Savannah needed a break from school before she starts kindergarten in the fall. I wanted to be able to spend more time with both of them."

The two women chatted for half an hour. When they learned that they were each the youngest child in their families, they laughed over the trials and tribulations of coping with bossy older brothers and sisters.


Caroline had been enjoying herself so much in spite of Derek's presence that she was unprepared for any discord. By late afternoon most of the guests had left. Ian's parents and grandmother had settled in the family room with Blake and Savannah, leaving the younger people gathered on the upper deck. When evening came, the only guests still present were Angela, Vanessa, Caroline and Keisha. The conversation turned to their days at college. They laughed and joked about the events they recalled from years earler. Their pleasant reminiscences were interrupted by Derek.

Looking directly at Caroline, he commented, "It's funny how people become very selective about what events they remember."

Keisha was oblivious to the undercurrent in his words. "What do you mean?"

"What I mean is that people give the impression that college was a totally enjoyable experience, that the people were like one big happy family. They seem to forget the unpleasant events and people.''

Unlike Keisha, Zoe felt that there was a specific reason for Derek's remark. She was determined to forestall an exchange that could become unpleasant. She turned her gaze on Derek.

''I don't think people necessarily forget bad experiences. There are probably times that they discuss their past problems with close friends.'' She smiled in an attempt to lighten the mood. ''And I'm sure we've all discussed some of our less friendly acquaintances. It's only normal not to dwell on either the bad events or the unpleasant people. I don't see that as a problem.''

A few seconds of silence followed. Despite Zoe's attempt to gloss over Derek's comment, everyone was feeling a little uncomfortable. Ian broke the silence.

''Would anyone like another drink?''

Vanessa took his question as a cue. ''No, thanks, Ian. If Caroline's ready, I think we'll be leaving.''

Caroline nodded and rose from her chair. She walked over to Zoe, who stood up as she approached. The two women embraced.

''Thanks for inviting me, Zoe. I enjoyed myself.''

Zoe looked uncertain.

Caroline smiled. ''I did enjoy the afternoon,'' she assured her.

''I'm glad. You and I will have to get together again while you're here. I'll give you a call. Maybe we can have lunch one day.''

Keisha and Angela also rose to leave. After seeing her guests out, Zoe returned and began helping Ian and Derek carry the remaining food to the kitchen. After her first trip from the deck to the kitchen she stayed in the house, putting away the leftovers.

Ian went to check on the children and Derek entered the kitchen with the last items cleared from the table on the deck. After depositing the tray on the counter, he turned to go. Zoe stopped him.

"Derek, I don't appreciate what happened out there a few minutes ago."

He turned around to face her. "What do you mean?"

"I mean that remark you made to Caroline. She was a guest in my home and you came very close to insulting her."

"I made a simple observation," he insisted.

"You made a statement full of innuendo and it was obvious that you directed it at her."

Derek opened his mouth to deny her accusation, but she raised her hand to stop him. "No, let me finish. I don't know what happened between the two of you years ago and I don't care. It's none of my business.

"What is my business is that Caroline was my guest and I didn't like having her treated that way by another guest— no, not just another guest, but a member of the family who's supposed to be helping to make the guests feel at home. Instead, you seemed to go out of your way to make her feel uncomfortable and I don't appreciate it. You may not have noticed, but Caroline wasn't the only one you made feel uncomfortable."

Placing her hand on her hip, she continued. "Whatever happened between the two of you is obviously still bothering you. I suggest that it's time for you to take her aside and discuss it instead of making snide remarks in front of strangers. If you're unable, or unwilling, to do that then all I can say is the best thing for you to do is get over it and let it go."

"Are you finished?"

Zoe lowered her hand from her hip and took a deep breath.

She walked around the counter and stopped directly in front of him.

"Just one more thing. I remember how kind you've always been to me, even years ago when things weren't so great between Ian and me. That's not the person I saw today."

She reached up and pulled his head down to plant a kiss on his cheek. "Whatever it is that's bothering you, don't let it change that kind, caring person I've known for years."

Derek was so surprised at the sudden change in her attitude, he could think of nothing to say. He turned and walked out the door.

A few minutes later, Ian entered the kitchen with a slight frown on his face. "What did you say to Derek?"

"What makes you think I said anything to him except to tell him good night?"

Ian moved forward and wrapped his arms around her. He kissed her forehead before leaning back to look her in the eye.

"For one thing, the look on his face. For another, I know you. I know you well enough to know that you wouldn't be content with your attempt to smooth over the comment he made out there on the deck."

Zoe repeated what she had said to her brother-in-law. "I couldn't leave his remark hanging in the air. It was just vague enough for everyone to wonder about the underlying reason for it. I didn't want to give anyone a chance to question him for further explanations."

She shook her head. "I can't say I'm sorry I said it, but I hope it doesn't cause any friction between the two of you."

"Don't worry about that. Derek and I long ago decided that there would be times when we would have to just agree to disagree. Whatever you discussed is between you."

"I'm glad to hear that. I guess he'll still be speaking to you then. I'm not so sure about me."

"I think you're underestimating him. I'm sure he's a bigger person than that."

"I hope you're right. He was pretty angry with me and I'm not sure my last words did much to soften that anger. He didn't say anything, but I could tell from the look on his face that he was probably counting to a hundred to keep from exploding."

Zoe had misjudged him. Derek was more surprised than angry at his sister-in-law's tongue lashing. Even before she chastised him, he regretted his actions. He was wrong to verbally attack Caroline in front of the others, but once he had uttered his statement, he was compelled to defend it.

He vowed that he would avoid any further outward show of animosity. As for Zoe's suggestion that he discuss his grievance with Caroline, he set that idea aside. He doubted that he could have such a discussion calmly and rationally. His only alternative was to avoid Caroline altogether. With her working at the center and the growing friendship between her and Zoe, that might be easier said than done.

# Chapter Six

After his decision to avoid Caroline, Derek realized that avoiding a physical meeting was the easy part. Even if she was at the center when he arrived, her classroom door was usually closed.

Eliminating her from his thoughts was more difficult. Even more bothersome was the fact that he had been unable to put Zoe's suggestion out of his mind.

It was still on his mind a week later, when the company had its monthly staff meeting. After the meeting, he and Ian adjourned to Ian's office to go over a contract that had been offered to the company. Ian sat behind the desk while Derek took a seat across from him. For the next half hour, they discussed the document.

When they had finished, Derek stood up and started toward the door. He had only taken a few steps before turning back to face his brother.

"I guess Zoe told you about our conversation the day of

the barbecue, though it wasn't much of a conversation. Mostly, I listened while she gave me a piece of her mind."

Ian nodded. "Yes, she told me. She was concerned that her comments to you might cause some tension between us."

Derek frowned. "You're kidding. She really thought that? What did you tell her?"

Ian shrugged. "I told her that our friendship doesn't depend on our agreeing about everything, and that your discussion is between you two."

Derek nodded. "I'm glad to hear you say that, but it sounds like you agree with what she said."

Ian rubbed his chin, gazing steadily at his brother. "Since you brought up the subject, yes, I agree."

Derek sighed. "I guess that doesn't really surprise me."

Ian cleared his throat. "You never told me what happened when you two broke up, Derek, but whatever it was, it's clear that it still bothers you. Don't you think it's time to put it behind you, to forget it?"

Derek shook his head. "It's not that easy to forget."

"Then confront her. Get it off your chest."

"I'm not sure I can do that without losing my temper."

Ian took a deep breath and leaned back in his chair. "Derek, I know you. You don't lose your temper easily. What could she possibly have done to make you so angry that you still have such resentment? It's been—what—six or seven years?"

Derek hesitated a moment before returning to his seat. He placed his hands on his knees, clasping them tightly as if it would help him hold his emotions in check.

"It was six years in May, but I can't forget what she did. She killed my child, our child," he said, his voice almost a whisper.

Ian sat up straight. "She *what?* I can't believe Caroline

is guilty of what you're saying. What child? How could you have kept this a secret all these years?''

Derek rubbed the back of his neck. ''It's not what you're thinking. She had an abortion.''

''And you didn't agree with her decision. Did you suggest an alternative?''

Derek stood up and began pacing. ''She didn't give me a chance to suggest anything. She didn't even discuss it with me.''

''You mean you didn't know she was pregnant until after she'd had the abortion?''

Derek faced Ian and nodded. ''That's right.''

Ian let out a long breath. He could well imagine his brother's anguish. He set aside the memories that flooded his mind and returned to the matter at hand.

''What reason did she give for not telling you she was pregnant?''

''She never gave me a reason.''

Ian was confused. Getting the whole story from his brother was like pulling teeth.

''I don't understand, Derek. What did she say when she told you about the abortion?''

''She didn't tell me. I overheard a conversation between two of her classmates.''

Ian stared at his brother and shook his head. ''Are you telling me that you never discussed it with her? How could you not ask her about it?''

''I called her with the intention of discussing it. I told her we needed to talk and she informed me that she didn't think we should see each other anymore.''

''And you let it go at that.''

He stopped pacing and sat down again. ''What would have been the point in going any further? The damage was already done. Besides, graduation was a month later. I never saw or spoke to her again, until I ran into her in Connecticut.''

"You never told me you saw her when you were in Connecticut. Did you talk to her?"

"Only briefly." Derek told him about their chance meeting at the hotel and his insistence that he drive her home. "Seeing her was such a shock that I didn't think about it at first."

"And later?"

Derek shrugged. "It was a short drive and not a very pleasant one. We didn't have much of a conversation at all. When I dropped her off at her house, I thought that was the end of it."

"But that wasn't the end of it. I imagine seeing her at the center was another shock."

Derek grunted and shook his head. "That's probably the understatement of the year."

Ian leaned forward, his forearms resting on the desk as he gazed at his brother. "There's something else that bothers me about this whole situation, Derek."

"What's that?"

"I can imagine how upset you were, but you overlooked one possible explanation. You based your belief on a conversation you overheard without insisting on discussing it with her or even asking her if it was true?"

"How would anyone even know there was a possibility that she could be pregnant? The only person she might have told would be Vanessa and I can't believe she would be responsible for such a rumor."

"They wouldn't have to know anything for sure. Some people just enjoy speculating about other people's lives, especially if their own lives are lacking in some way. If it was deliberately malicious, the purpose might have been to plant a seed of doubt in your mind. If there was no chance the child was yours, maybe they wanted you to think she was having an affair with someone else.''

''You're reaching for an excuse for her, Ian.''

Ian shrugged. ''Maybe, but think about it. Given some of the hateful things people do, it's not that farfetched.''

''What possible reason would they have to lie? I can't imagine that anyone hated Caroline enough to start such a rumor.''

Ian shook his head. ''I don't know the answer to that. I'm not even saying they were lying, or at least not as they would see it. Who knows how the rumor started or who actually started it? I'm just saying that until you ask her, she deserves the benefit of the doubt.''

Derek was silent. He had never before considered the chance that the conversation he had overheard was simply another of the rumors that seem to abound on most campuses. He certainly would never have considered that it was done maliciously.

Ian knew he had given his brother disturbing food for thought, but he continued to press his point. ''Do you recall a conversation that we had a few years ago when you were urging me to confront Zoe about our relationship?''

Derek nodded.

''The shoe's on the other foot now. You owe it to Caroline to find out the truth. More importantly, you owe to yourself. If you haven't put this behind you by now, chances are you never will until you confront her. If it's true, you'll have to find a way to overcome the anger. If it's not true . . . well, that's a whole different situation.''


A few days after the barbecue, Zoe telephoned Caroline. Since their first meeting at the center, she had hoped the two of them would have an opportunity to become better acquainted. That had been one of her reasons for inviting Caroline to the party.

Zoe was now wary of how Caroline might respond to her invitation. The little she knew of Caroline suggested that she was not the kind of person who would harbor ill feelings toward Zoe because of Derek's remark. Many people believed in guilt by association and Zoe might be mistaken in her assessment of Caroline's ability to remain objective.

"Hi, Caroline, I hope I'm not calling too early."

"Hi, Zoe. No, it's not too early. I've been up for a couple of hours."

"I called to see if you'd like to have lunch with me on Saturday?"

"Sure, I don't have any other plans. Where, and what time shall I meet you?"

"Since you're not very familiar with the area, why don't I pick you up, say, twelve-thirty?"

"That sounds fine."

"Good, I'll see you Saturday."

Zoe arrived almost fifteen minutes late. Caroline had spied the car from the living room window and went to open the door before Zoe had a chance to ring the bell.

"I'm sorry I'm late. Savannah decided she had a big emergency just as I was leaving."

Once they were settled in the car, Zoe turned to Caroline. "I thought we'd go someplace simple. Maybe afterward we'll have time for some shopping, if you're interested."

Caroline laughed. "I think I could manage to drum up a little enthusiasm for that."

\* \* \*

Halfway through lunch, Zoe asked, "How are you managing at the center?"

"Fine. I like the fact that Angela recruited some of the older students to help."

Zoe nodded. "They started out as volunteers. It's great that she has the funds to pay them now. Most of them need the money. The families get by okay as a rule, but the job gives the kids money for extras that their parents can't afford."

Center activities remained the topic of conversation for the remainder of the meal. During their drive to the mall, Zoe recalled Caroline's comment about her nephew and the conversation turned to their respective families.

"Is your family nearby?" Caroline asked.

"No, they're all in Pennsylvania. I stayed here in Georgia after I finished college. My mother wasn't happy with that decision, but I was determined to prove that I could make it on my own. We both know how some parents have a tendency to be overprotective with the youngest child. On top of that, you have to contend with older brothers and sisters who think they're your parents."

Caroline nodded. "I managed to assert my independence without moving far away. It wasn't easy, though. You said your family's in Pennsylvania. What part?"

"Philadelphia, mostly, but I have a brother in Pittsburgh."

Caroline laughed. "I can't believe it! That's where Jason—my oldest brother—lives. Well, actually, he lives in a suburb of Pittsburgh. He's the one with the little boy who just turned two." Just then they arrived at Lenox Square, and conversation took a backseat to shopping.

For almost two weeks after his disturbing conversation with Ian, Derek mulled over his brother's words. Ian's argu-

ments were valid. Derek had been shocked when he overheard the two women discussing Caroline's supposed
abortion. His initial disbelief should have convinced him
that he needed to hear Caroline's explanation. In his own
defense, he had tried to talk to her afterward. She was the
one who had abruptly cut him off before he could question
her further.

Until a few months ago, he was convinced that the pain
of the events surrounding their breakup was behind him. He
knew now that that was a lie. The truth had taken him
completely by surprise when he came face to face with
Caroline after so many years. As much as he hated to admit
it, Ian and Zoe were right. He would never be satisfied until
he confronted her.

Derek had spotted Caroline a few times when she was
leaving as he arrived at the center. He had come close to
approaching her but when she saw him, she turned away
and hurried to her car. It was clear that she had no desire
to hear anything he had to say.

He had no choice but to force the issue. It was time to
have the talk they should have had a long time ago. He
considered going directly to Vanessa's house in the evening.
He had no intention of calling first and giving her the opportunity to refuse to see him. The problem with arriving unan-
nounced was that she might not be there. He would hate to
gear himself up for this discussion and have to postpone it.
Besides, they needed privacy. Zoe had made that point clear.

He would approach her at the center. They could decide
where to go from there. He would make it impossible for
her to ignore him, although she still might refuse to talk to
him at all. He timed his visit for late in the afternoon, after
the students had gone home. Caroline was likely to be there,
putting the classroom in order.

* * *

Caroline had no idea Derek was deliberately avoiding her, but she was glad that she had had no close encounter with him since the barbecue. The few times she had noticed him as she was leaving, she had avoided any eye contact. Her efforts at avoiding him had not kept him from her mind, though.

She had given a great deal of thought to his veiled remark at the barbecue. Neither she nor Vanessa could understand his animosity. It was hard to believe he was still so angry simply because she had broken up with him years ago.

There was only one other possibility that she could imagine, now that she knew he wasn't married. When Marquita had found out he was dating Caroline, she would have been angry. Maybe she had broken off the engagement as a result of that discovery. After giving the idea more thought, Caroline discarded it. Marquita had given Caroline no indication that she planned to break off her engagement. Whatever the reason for Derek's anger, she was determined not to let him ruin her summer.

He had been so much on her mind, she almost believed her thoughts had conjured him up in the flesh when he walked into the classroom. She murmured a greeting and continued filing papers into her totebag.

"Caroline, I guess I should start by apologizing for the comments I made at the barbecue."

Caroline glanced at him. He seemed to be sincere, but she was still wary.

"I accept your apology."

She held her breath, waiting for him to leave the room. She looked around, ostensibly to assure herself that the students had left no personal items behind. She turned to face him when he spoke again.

"I had no right to air personal issues in front of the other guests." He glanced toward the door. "We do need to talk, but I don't think this setting is much better than the party would have been for having a private discussion."

"What, exactly, are you suggesting, Derek? I can't believe that we have anything that important to discuss after all these years."

Derek rubbed the back of his neck. "I guess you think I'm being unnecessarily cryptic. Believe me, Caroline, it's important."

Caroline sighed. "If you feel that strongly, I guess we could go back to Vanessa's house. She won't be home from work for at least a couple of hours."

Derek nodded. "I'll follow you."

For the entire trip, Caroline went over and over in her mind their brief conversation. She questioned her decision to agree to this meeting. She could have simply refused his request. In fact, that had been her first inclination. The fact that it was a request and that he appeared to be genuinely apologetic weighed heavily in her agreement to talk to him. Curiosity was another reason. She had to know what was so important after all these years that they had to discuss it in private.

When she let herself into Vanessa's house, Derek was right behind her. "Would you like a drink?" she asked, setting her bag and purse on the hall table. "There's some iced tea and lemonade. I think there are a few sodas, too."

Derek nodded. "Iced tea sounds fine, thanks." He followed her to the kitchen and took a seat at the small table, silently watching her. It seemed to him that she took an inordinately long time with her preparations.

"How are the classes going?"

"Fine. Zoe had already established a routine that works

well. The older students have been very helpful in working with the younger ones.''

Caroline was not eager to dissect what had occurred so many years ago. Did he think she was totally unaware of his deception? Why did he insist on opening an old wound? It had taken years for that wound to heal. Lately, she questioned whether it had healed at all.

She went along with his diversionary comments, and for a few minutes they discussed the center and its programs while she took two glasses from the cupboard and filled them with ice. After setting them on the counter, she retrieved a pitcher from the refrigerator and filled both glasses. She carried them to the table and took a seat across from him.

Caroline went straight to the point. ''What did you want to talk to me about, Derek?''

Derek was not as direct. He sipped his iced tea slowly, searching for the right words.

''Something we should have discussed years ago. All this time I thought I'd put it behind me. In the last few months, and especially the last few weeks, I've realized that's not true.''

Caroline was almost sure what he meant. She still found it hard to believe he was upset about a breakup that took place over six years ago, but she had to ask.

''You're being cryptic again, Derek. What's this about?''

''Why did you end our relationship, Caroline?''

She stood up and went to refrigerator. ''Why does that concern you so much now?'' she asked, taking a bowl of lemon wedges from the shelf.

Before he could answer her question, she turned to face him, shaking her head. ''Never mind that. I can't believe you're even asking me that question. What did you expect me to do, Derek? Did you expect me to continue seeing you when I found out that you were engaged to another woman?

You must have known that I'd eventually find out about her when she returned to Atlanta.''

Derek frowned. "I don't know what you're talking about. I wasn't engaged."

"Look, Derek, if you, or she, broke the engagement when she came back to Atlanta, it doesn't matter. You were engaged when we were seeing each other."

"Caroline, I wasn't engaged before, during, or after our relationship. Where did you get this information?"

"From the horse's mouth, so to speak. Marquita, your fiancée, told me."

"Marquita Edwards?"

Caroline nodded, turning back to the counter and dropping one of the wedges into her glass. "She even showed me the ring."

He shook his head. "I've never been engaged to Marquita Edwards."

"Then why didn't you ask me why I didn't want to see you again? If it bothers you so much now, you should have cared enough to ask that question years ago."

Derek considered her statement about Marquita. If she'd thought that he was engaged, he could understand why she might feel forced into ridding herself of their child.

"I assumed you were ending our relationship because you were afraid I'd find out about the abortion."

Caroline spun around. Her mouth dropped open. "The *what?*"

"The abortion."

Forgetting the iced tea, Caroline returned to the table, where Derek sat tightly clasping his glass with both hands. She leaned over, placing her hands on the table.

"What gave you the idea I'd had an abortion? I told you I wasn't pregnant a month before that."

He shook his head. "No, you didn't. What you said was there was no reason to be worried."

"How in the world did that lead you to the conclusion that I'd had an abortion?"

"That statement only reinforced what I already suspected. I overheard two of your classmates talking about it."

Caroline frowned. "You heard someone say that I'd had an abortion? Who?"

Derek shrugged. "I didn't really know them. I think one of them was Barbara something-or-other. What difference does it make who they were?"

She remembered a girl named Barbara Ormsby from one of her classes. She had always had some sarcastic remark to make and it was always directed at Caroline. Caroline discovered the reason for her snide comments when Marquita told her about her supposed engagement. Barbara had been at Marquita's side with a smirk on her face.

Caroline let out a long breath. "You overheard a statement made by someone you didn't know, a person you knew wasn't even a friend of mine, and you assumed that what she said about me was true."

Her voice became louder. "That was enough for you to doubt my integrity, to believe that I would make a decision to abort our child without even discussing it with you. How could you?"

He rubbed his neck. "I didn't see any reason someone would lie about it, but if you recall, I tried to talk to you. When I called you, you were so abrupt I thought you must be hiding something from me."

At the time that had seemed a reasonable conclusion. He knew now that it was a weak excuse, but he had no other answer to her question.

"I refused to talk to you because I didn't want to hear your excuses for not telling me about Marquita."

"I'll say it again. I was not, nor have I ever been engaged to Marquita Edwards, or anyone else."

Caroline sank down onto the chair, her shoulders sagging. "If you say so, Derek. That doesn't erase your willingness to believe that I'd be underhanded enough to have an abortion without even discussing it with you."

He opened his mouth to speak, although he had no idea what he could say to make her see the situation from his viewpoint. Before he could formulate an excuse, Caroline spoke again.

"I think you'd better leave, Derek. You've gotten your answers. I don't think there's anything more for us to discuss."

She rose from her seat and walked over to the sink, staring out of the window. She stood there with her back to him, silently willing him to leave.

Derek watched in silence. Ian had tried to warn him that there was a chance he was basing his assumptions on a rumor. He had trouble understanding why someone would spread such a hateful lie. She had not turned to face him and it was obvious she had no intention of continuing the conversation. He stood up and started toward her.

Caroline stiffened slightly when she sensed him standing behind her. Still, she did not turn to face him.

Derek sighed. "Good night, Caroline," he murmured. Then he turned and walked away.

Caroline heard the door close behind him. Her shoulders slumped and a tear trickled down her cheek. She absently wiped it away as she picked up the glass on the counter and poured her tea down the drain.

# Chapter Seven

Sharmane slowly backed out of the garage and came to an abrupt stop when she noticed the car blocking the driveway. Her heartbeat quickened when a man stepped out of the car and started up the driveway. What was he doing here? She knew he had been released from prison, but she never expected to see him again.

In fact, she had hoped never to see him again. It had taken her years to put her life back together. What would she do if he wanted her back?

As he neared her car, she reluctantly rolled down the driver-side window. Whatever his reason for coming, he had given her no choice but to hear him out.

"Hello, Sharmane," he murmured, placing his hands on the side of the car.

Sharmane licked her lips nervously. "Hello, Cal. What brings you here?"

"I'm not here to bother you, Sharmane. There's no reason

for you to be afraid of me. In fact, I came to let you know that I plan to repay the money you put up for legal fees.''

"That's not necessary, Cal. After all, you were my husband. It was the least I could do.''

Cal stood up straight and took a step back. "*Were* being the operative word.''

Sharmane's eyes widened slightly. Her hands tightened on the steering wheel. She had loved him once. When he was arrested, she stood by him. Later, her discovery of all that he had done had been the beginning of the slow death of that love. The fact that he had been totally unrepentant had sealed her decision to file for divorce.

"I don't blame you for divorcing me, Sharmane. And I told you, you have no reason to be afraid of me. I just wanted to see you again and to let you know that you'll get your money back.''

Sharmane nodded. "If you insist.'' She loosened her grip on the steering wheel. "I'm really sorry about your mother, Cal.''

He took a deep breath. "Thanks. I got your letter after the funeral.'' He took another step back. "I'll move the car so you can be on your way. Good-bye, Sharmane.''

Sharmane watched in the rearview mirror as he returned to his car. A moment later, he drove off without another glance in her direction.

He had assured her that she was in no danger from him. She wanted to believe that. Deep down, she did believe it. His anger had never been directed toward her. She was not deceived by his calm demeanor, though. He was angry.

Through his rearview mirror, Cal watched her back out of the driveway as he drove slowly down the street. He wondered if she had moved from the house they had shared in an effort to keep him from finding her or if it was because she could no longer afford to live there.

It was clear she no longer trusted him, but he held no animosity toward her. That emotion was reserved for Ian. He was the one to blame for everything, including his mother's death. She had had a weak heart for years. That last heart attack was too much.

His attorney had had to beg the prison authorities to allow him to attend his own mother's funeral. Ian had had the good sense to absent himself from that event, but his parents had been there. They had even had the nerve to approach him and offer their condolences. If he had his way, they soon would be on the receiving end of such sentiments.

After leaving Sharmane, Cal drove to one of the monthly meetings he had been attending since shortly after his release. His attorney had suggested he could help the young probationers who had been involved in petty crimes. It was clear that, unless they changed, they were bound to end up in prison for more serious offenses.

Cal's part was to make them aware that losing their freedom was a high price to pay in itself. Other ex-convicts were there to paint the more sordid picture of a maximum-security prison.

After the first meeting, Cal realized the meetings could serve a useful purpose for his future plans.

He entered the meeting room now and looked around. He had been watching the participants carefully, one young man in particular. It was obvious that D.C. was only there because it was a condition of his probation. Cal decided it was time to feel him out.

After the meeting, he approached D.C. "So what do think of these meetings?"

D.C.'s eyes narrowed. "Why you wanna know?"

Cal shrugged. "Because you don't seem to be all that

interested in plodding along in a regular job. I might be able to help you earn some real money. You interested?''

"You don't want me to off nobody, do you?''

Cal shook his head. "No, nothing like that. It's a very simple job, really. I need two people, though.''

D.C. cocked his head to one side. "How much money you talkin' about.''

"Fifty thousand dollars—each.''

D.C.'s eyes widened. "You serious, man? And I don't have to off nobody?''

"That's right. So, are you interested or not.''

D.C. nodded. "Yeah, man, and I got a friend who'll want in on this.''

"Can you vouch for this friend keeping his mouth shut?''

"Yeah.'' D.C. laughed. "For that kind of dough, he'll keep his mouth shut.''

Cal set up a meeting place and time. "Bring your friend with you.''

The smirk on Cal's face as he drove away from the meeting was one of total satisfaction. His plans were coming together. He had had Ian and Zoe under surveillance for months. It seemed that he had just found the only missing piece in his preparations for revenge.

The money was an important factor in that revenge, but imagining Ian's fear was the real satisfaction. Losing his wife forever would be an even greater revenge, but Cal was still undecided about taking that step.


Sharmane's conversation with Cal stayed on her mind for days after their meeting. She had been unable to shake the feeling of forboding.

Because of her preoccupation she had hesitated when Jeff

called suggesting dinner. He had been persistent and she had finally relented.

She admitted to herself that sitting at home stewing about Cal's motives was futile. Maybe dinner with Jeff would take her mind off her ex-husband.

Jeff had sensed she was upset when he spoke with her on the telephone. Watching her now, he frowned slightly. It went unnoticed by Sharmane, sitting on the opposite side of the table. He doubted she had heard anything he had said since the waiter had seated them.

"Are you still with me, Sharmane?" he asked.

Sharmane shoved aside the thoughts that had been churning in her mind and gave him her full attention. "I'm sorry, Jeff. I guess I'm not very good company tonight."

"What's wrong, sweetheart?"

"Nothing really," she insisted.

Jeff waited patiently for the truth.

Sharmane sighed. "I had a visit from Cal a few days ago."

"Cal?" His eyes narrowed. He had glimpsed a trace of fear in her eyes. "Did he threaten you?"

Sharmane laid her hand on top of his. "No, Jeff. He didn't threaten me. In fact, he made a point of telling me that he didn't blame me for dicorcing him."

"Then what are you afraid of?"

Sharmane's eyes widened. She should have known he would sense the emotion underneath her calm exterior.

"I'm not sure. I could tell he's still angry, but not with me. I just hope he doesn't do anything stupid."

"If he's not angry with you, why did he come to see you? What did he actually say to you?"

"Not much." She took a deep breath and shook her head slowly. "I think he came to say good-bye. That's what concerns me, and scares me a little."

Jeff clasped her hand in both of his. "Promise me something?"

Sharmane looked into his chocolate brown eyes, now filled with concern. "What?"

"If he calls you or comes to see you again, call me. If you can avoid it, don't see him again."

"Jeff, I told you he's not angry with me."

He nodded. "I know what you told me. I also know, from some other stories you've told me about him, that you can't trust him. So, will you promise to call me?"

Sharmane smiled for the first time that evening. "Yes, I promise."

Zoe had just put Savannah and Blake down for their naps when the telephone rang. Ian was on the other end.

"Hi, sweetheart. How was your morning?"

"Fine, we just got back a few minutes ago."

"Where are the kids?"

"Napping, or at least I hope they will be soon. I just put them down."

"That sounds like it'll fit in with my plans."

"What plans are those?"

"I was thinking about coming home for lunch."

"Do you want me to fix something for you?"

"As a matter of fact, yes."

"What would you like?"

"You. I've already eaten lunch. I'm looking for dessert."

Zoe chuckled. "I see. How soon will you be here?"

"I'll be there by the time the kids are asleep."

Twenty minutes later, Ian walked into their bedroom. Zoe was nowhere in sight, but the bed had been turned down. He locked the door and sat down on the side of the bed. He had only removed his shoes when Zoe entered from the bathroom dressed in a silk robe.

She walked over to him and began unbuttoning his shirt. "Can I expect this to become a regular occurrence now that I'm no longer spending my afternoons at the center?"

"Hmmm, I hadn't really thought that far ahead, but it sounds like a great idea."

He stood up and shrugged out of his shirt as she undid the hook on his slacks and began easing down the zipper. He took a deep breath when she slid her hand into the opening.

She removed her hand and, hooking her thumbs in the waist of his slacks, pushed them down to his knees. She started to perform the same task with his briefs, but was sidetracked when he loosened the belt of her robe and it fell open.

His hand captured one breast and began gently kneading it. His other arm encircled her waist, pulling her close. He kicked his legs free of the slacks as their lips met. With a little help from him, her robe slipped from her shoulders and pooled at her feet. His hands roamed up and down her body.

"I could easily make this a habit," he murmured against her lips.

"I agree. There's something a little wanton about making love in the middle of the afternoon. Especially when there's a curious little girl in the house."

"That part might not be such a problem if a certain person was a little quieter with her expressions of appreciation," Ian commented, easing her onto the bed.

He quickly disposed of his briefs and lay down beside her. He continued his pleasant torture, caressing and exploring every inch of her body.

Zoe reached over and grasped his shoulder. "I want you now, Ian."

Positioning himself between her soft thighs, he murmured, "Soon, baby, soon."

Her scent enveloped him. He kissed her again as he entered her hot, moist sheath. "You feel so good. I'll never get enough of you."

Zoe moaned as he moved inside her. Her hands slid down his back, finally clasping and kneading the flexing muscles of his buttocks.

They moved together, as they had so many times before. Lost in the sensations that washed over them and the passion that consumed them, they were oblivious to everything except each other.

Zoe wrapped her legs around him, urging him deeper. She gasped when she felt the first tremors of ecstasy. As her body contracted in pleasure, it drove Ian over the edge and together they reached the pinnacle of rapture.

They lay there for a few minutes afterward, basking in the glow of sated passion. Ian was the first to speak.

"As much as I'd like to stay right here for the rest of the day, I guess I'd better get back to the office."

Zoe leaned up on her elbow and began drawing circles on his chest. "Why? You're the president of the company. Take the rest of the day off."

Ian chuckled. "You have a point, but it never seems to work that way."

He stilled her hand. Then he sighed and sat up, swinging his legs around to sit on the side of the bed. After leaning over to plant one last kiss on her lips, he stood up and started toward the bathroom.

Zoe watched him, smiling in admiration at the physique she knew in intimate detail. Her grin broadened at the idea of joining him in the shower, which might just keep him

home for the rest of the afternoon. She glanced at the clock
and sighed. She might be able to count on Blake sleeping
for a few hours, but Savannah would probably be up in
another half hour. She reluctantly set aside her plan to join
Ian.

At dinner that evening, Zoe was still thinking about her
lunchtime visit from her husband. Halfway through the meal
her attention was drawn to her daughter.

"Stop playing with your food, Savannah. If you don't
want anymore, just say so."

"Can I have dessert?"

Zoe shook her head at her daughter's audacity.

Ian sighed. "You mean, 'may I have dessert,' and you
know the rules. If you don't eat your vegetables and drink
your milk, no dessert."

Ian almost choked on his water at Zoe's next remark,
directed at him. "Did you eat all your vegetables at lunch
today?" she murmured under her breath.

He grinned. "As a matter of fact, I did. I knew I'd need
strength and stamina to do justice to my 'dessert.' "

Their remarks had gone unnoticed by Savannah, who was
still trying to decide if she wanted dessert. Finally, she
slowly resumed eating.

"Mommy took us to the zoo today, Daddy. I petted the
lambs and the goats."

"Did you enjoy it?"

She wrinkled her nose. "The goats didn't smell good, but
it was fun. Blake liked it, too. He was too little to ride the
pony, though."

Ian stifled a chuckle. "Well, I'm glad you had fun."

# Chapter Eight

In the week following their disturbing confrontation, Caroline did not encounter Derek at the center, but their conversation at Vanessa's house was always in the back of her mind. She had told Vanessa nothing of Derek's visit and their conversation. By the time her friend arrived at home, she had washed her face and regained her composure. When Vanessa commented on her lack of appetite at dinner, Caroline gave her the excuse of having eaten a big lunch. Pleading a headache, she had retired to her room early that evening.

Caroline and Derek had reached no solution to their misunderstanding. She doubted that there could be a resolution, and she had no desire to delve deeper into that painful memory. What possible excuse could he offer for his perception of her as deceitful and underhanded? She just wanted to forget the entire episode.

A week after their conversation, Caroline arrived at the

center to be informed by Rita that Angela wanted to see her. She knocked on the office door and entered.

"Hi, Angela, Rita said you wanted to see me."

"Hi, Caroline. I have a favor to ask. I have a meeting with one of our benefactors this afternoon and I'm not sure I'll be back in time to close up. I'd ask Rita to stay, but she has to take her daughter to the dentist. Would you mind locking up after your class?"

"No problem," Caroline assured her.


At four o'clock that afternoon, Caroline instructed the students to put away their books and papers and she joined Rita at the reception desk. "I'll take over here, Rita. The kids should be leaving soon."

Ten minutes later, the last student had left and Caroline was preparing to lock up when a man entered. He swaggered over to the desk and leaned on the counter.

"I'm here for my daughter, Terita Conyers."

"I'm sorry, Mr. Conyers, all of the children have left."

"I don't believe you. Where is she?"

Caroline smelled the alcohol on his breath as he leaned over the counter. That, and his belligerent attitude, struck a chord in Caroline's mind. Angela had warned her about this man.

The center employees had specific instructions that he was not to be allowed on the premises. He had caused problems in the past.

"I told you she's not here. Even if she was here, I couldn't let her go with you." Too late, she realized that her last statement might antagonize him.

"What do you mean you can't let her go with me? I'm her father." He started toward the back of the center. "I'll find her myself."

Caroline came from behind the counter to head him off. "You can't go back there, Mr. Conyers. I told you your daughter isn't here."

At that moment, Derek came through the door carrying a large carton. "What's the problem?"

Conyers turned around to face him. "Who are you?"

Setting the box on the counter, Derek replied, "I think I should be asking you that question."

"I'm here to get my daughter."

Caroline spoke up. "This is Mr. Conyers. I explained to him that the children had left. I was just getting ready to lock up."

"Where's Angela?" he asked, glancing toward her office.

"She had to leave early."

"I think you'd better leave, too, Mr. Conyers."

"I ain't goin' nowhere without my kid."

"Caroline, call nine-one-one."

She started past the intruder to get to the telephone and he grabbed her arm. Before Derek could act, Caroline smashed her fist into Conyers's nose and her knee came up to catch him in the groin. He doubled over in pain and staggered back. When he started toward her again, Derek grabbed him.

"Caroline, call nine-one-one. Mr. Conyers, I think you'd be wise to leave, now."

Derek let go of the other man whose gaze wavered between him and Caroline, who had returned to her former station behind the counter. She picked up the telephone receiver and Conyers headed toward the door. Derek followed him and locked the door.

Caroline sank down onto the chair, willing her heart beat to slow down. She was still trying to calm her nerves when Derek returned and knelt down in front of her.

"Are you all right?"

She nodded. "I'm fine," she insisted, examining her fist, which was sore from punching Conyers.

"I doubt that." He stood up and left her for a few minutes, returning with a cup of water.

"You could probably use something a lot stronger, but this will have to do."

When Caroline took the paper cup from his hand, their fingers touched, sending a shiver through her that had nothing to do with her encounter with Mr. Conyers. She sipped the water slowly while he stood watching her. When she finished, she looked around for a trash can. Derek held out his hand and she gave him the empty cup.

"Thanks."

He touched her shoulder. "Come on. It's time to go home."

She stood up and left the reception cubicle, heading toward Angela's office.

"Where are you going?"

"I have to get my purse from the locker."

He followed her, watching from the doorway as she retrieved her purse. They turned to leave and he noticed the box still sitting on the counter.

"Wait for me while I put these scanners in the back. I don't want you going out alone, just in case our friend is still hanging around out there."

He returned a few minutes later. They left together and Derek set the alarm. When they reached her car, he waited until she was behind the wheel.

"I'll follow you home—to Vanessa's."

"You don't have to do that. I'm fine."

"I'll follow you anyway."

\* \* \*

When she arrived at Vanessa's house, Caroline parked the car at the curb and got out. Derek pulled his car into the space behind hers and walked with her to the door. She let herself into the house and turned to face him.

"Thank you."

"May I come in?"

Caroline could guess why he wanted to come in. She had no desire to take up where they had left off in their previous encounter, but refusing his request would be rude. Considering he had come to her aid just a short time earlier, she supposed she owed him that courtesy. Whatever he had to add to the explanation she had already heard, she could hear him out without responding.

"Sure. Would you care for a drink?"

Derek nodded and followed her to the kitchen. Taking the same seat he had occupied a week earlier, he waited patiently while she prepared drinks for both of them.

He had been unable to get her out of his mind since their last meeting. The anger and pain in her eyes after his accusation, had haunted him all week. He now wondered how he could have accused her of such deceit, especially based on so flimsy an excuse. At least the information that had led her to believe he was engaged had come directly from the person involved, unlike his own assumptions.

Caroline experienced a moment of déjà vu as she repeated the same preparations she had followed the previous week. She poured the tea and carried the glasses to the table. Their gazes met when she set them on the table.

"Where did you learn to do that?"

Caroline's mind was still on their previous conversation and the likelihood that he planned to continue the discussion. She frowned.

"Do what?"

"What you did to Mr. Conyers when he grabbed your arm."

She shrugged. "I took a self-defense course about a year ago. I never had to use it before. I was never really sure I'd be able to do it, except in a practice situation, or that I'd even remember what to do."

"You did very well."

"I think it was probably just the fact that I had the element of surprise on my side."

He shook his head. "That might be part of it, but don't sell your abilities short. I'm sure his actions caught you by surprise, too, but you didn't freeze."

Caroline made no comment to that observation. She returned to the refrigerator and lifted the lemon wedges from the shelf. She set the bowl on the table, taking the seat across from him.

"You didn't have to follow me home," she insisted.

"Yes, I did. Whether you know it or not, or whether you're willing to admit it, you were still very shaky at the center."

They were both silent for a moment sipping their drinks. Her attention stayed focused on her glass when she broke the silence.

"Why are you here?"

He shrugged. "I told you, you were still shaky and I didn't feel comfortable letting you drive back here alone."

"You accomplished that when we reached the door. Why did you feel it necessary to come in?"

"We didn't finish our conversation the last time I was here. What you told me came as quite a surprise. I guess I have no one to blame but myself for not insisting that we settle the issue a long time ago. I've been thinking about it all week.

"Although I did try to talk to you at the time, I don't

blame you for being angry. I never thought you were deceitful, Caroline. I was angry and hurt. You were so abrupt when I called that I started to believe the story was true.''

''I was abrupt because I was angry. I had every reason to believe you had misled me and used me.''

''In other words, you believed that I was a deceitful manipulator.''

''I understand what you're getting at, Derek, but it's not the same thing.'' She picked up her glass, stood up and started toward the refrigerator to refill her glass.

Derek stood up at the same time and headed her off, standing directly in front of her. Taking the glass from her hand, he set it back on the table. Then he reached out and tilted her chin so she had to meet his gaze.

''I guess it's not the same in degrees. It is the same in that we're both guilty of believing lies and we were both hurt.''

''You said you and Marquita were never engaged.''

''That's right. The whole truth is that Marquita and I dated in high school and a few times when she was home from college during the summer. I haven't dated her at all since her junior year in college, years before I met you.''

Looking deep into his eyes had an hypnotic effect on Caroline. She had known this man intimately—emotionally and physically.

Until Marquita's accusation, she had never known him to be a liar. In fact, there had been times when he had been painfully honest. Those instances had been of minor importance, but she had always believed that if a person lied about big things they would lie about the little ones.

Unless he had become a consummate actor in the last six years, he was telling the truth. As confusing and upsetting as that possibility was, she believed him.

''But the ring . . .''

He took her hands in his. "Anyone can buy a ring, Caroline."

The combination of the sincerity in his voice, the look in his eyes, and that simple touch reminded Caroline of what they had shared years ago. She licked her lips. Then she cleared her throat and responded to his simple statement.

"It's hard to believe that someone would go to all that trouble. Lying to me about your relationship and buying a ring as proof seems so childish and ridiculous."

"That doesn't bother me as much as the thought that someone deliberately spread the rumor that you'd aborted our child. Marquita wasn't the one who told me that."

Caroline bit her lip. "No, she wouldn't be that open. I don't think she wanted you to know that she was aware of our relationship. She probably wouldn't be above having one of her friends see that the story got around, though. Her friend Barbara was with her when she told me she was engaged to you."

"She must have been the one I overheard."

Caroline shook her head. "But why? Just because of our relationship? What purpose did it serve? Did Marquita think you'd go running back to her? I'm sure I'm not the only woman you dated after you and she broke up."

"As for what purpose it served, it ended our relationship, didn't it? Maybe she did believe she and I would eventually get back together. I don't know. Whatever she heard about any other women I dated, she must have realized that none of them posed a threat. I was never serious about any of the other women."

His thumbs caressed the knuckles of her hands. "I'm sorry, Caroline. I'm sorry for the hurt you were caused, and I'm especially sorry about my part in contributing to that pain."

He took a deep breath. "I never stopped caring about you, in spite of everything."

"Derek . . ."

Before she could say another word, he dropped one of her hands and placed his finger on her lips, silencing her. "Let me finish. I'm not suggesting we pick up where we left off years ago. We can't undo what was done or take back the words, but we can agree that we were both misled and put it behind us for good.

"Seeing you again has made me realize how much you mean to me. I haven't been able to get you out of my mind since I saw you in Connecticut. I guess what I'm suggesting is that we start from now and see where it leads us."

He let go of her other hand. "Do you think we could do that? Or maybe I should ask if you're even willing to try?"

She clasped her hands together in front of her and focused her attention on them. "What do you mean by starting from now?"

He tipped her chin up, forcing to meet his gaze once again. "Have dinner with me tomorrow?"

That might have sounded harmless enough if she had not recognized in those eyes the desire that had been missing in their previous encounters. Or maybe she had been so angry she had overlooked it. In spite of some misgivings, she nodded. "Yes, I'll have dinner with you, Derek," she murmured, her voice little more than a whisper.

Any further conversation was interrupted by the arrival of Vanessa. She stopped abruptly when she reached the kitchen.

"Oh, hi, Derek."

"Hello, Vanessa," he murmured before turning his attention back to Caroline. "I'll see you tomorrow. Is seven o'clock okay?"

"Seven o'clock is fine." She glanced at Vanessa and turned again toward Derek. "I'll see you to the door."

When Caroline returned to the kitchen a few minutes later, Vanessa was pouring herself a glass of lemonade. She carried her glass to the table, sat down and turned her attention to her friend.

"Do you want to tell me what's going on? Or do you want to tell me to mind my own business?"

Caroline sat down across from her friend. "You know we've been good friends for too long for me to tell you to mind your own business. I'd end up telling you about it eventually, anyway. It might as well be now." She told Vanessa the whole story, starting with Derek's previous visit and the reason for it.

Vanessa almost choked on her lemonade. She set her glass on the table. "He actually accused you of secretly having an abortion?"

Caroline nodded. "Do you remember Barbara Ormsby?"

Vanessa frowned. "Oh yes, I remember Barbara Ormsby. I remember how hateful she was to you. What does she have to do with it?"

"Derek said he overheard two of our classmates discussing my 'abortion.' He didn't know them, but one was named Barbara 'something.' Considering she was Marquita's friend, Barbara Ormsby seems a likely suspect."

"And Derek swears he was never engaged to Marquita?"

Caroline nodded.

Vanessa focused her attention on her glass. "And you believe him?"

"Yes, Vanessa, I believe him. Not just because I want to believe him. What he said makes sense." She put her elbows on the table and rested her chin on her hands. "Do you remember how surprised Keisha was when you asked about Derek's wife?"

Vanessa looked up from her glass. She shrugged. "Yes, I remember."

"I know her statement that he doesn't have a wife doesn't prove that he's never been married, or engaged. Considering her reaction to your question and putting all the other pieces together, I have to give him the benefit of the doubt."

Vanessa swirled the ice around in her glass. She took a sip and smiled. "Is that what you were doing today? Giving him the benefit of the doubt?"

Caroline grinned. "I guess you could say that, since I practically threw him out of the house the last time. He had wanted to continue the discussion then, but I didn't want to hear anything else after his accusation."

"So you told him you were ready to hear him out."

"Not exactly." She told her about the altercation with Mr. Conyers and Derek's insistence on following her home. "I could hardly refuse when he asked to come in."

Satisfied that Caroline was all right now, Vanessa nodded slowly and smiled again. "Of course not." She took another sip of lemonade. "Now what? Did I hear you mention something about tomorrow evening?"

"Yes, I'm having dinner with him tomorrow." She looked at her friend closely.

Vanessa reached across the table and patted her arm. "I'm happy for you, Caroline. Whatever happens, I'm glad you two finally cleared the air. It was long overdue. I just have one more question. Where do you go from here?"

"To dinner tomorrow."

"Very funny."

Caroline shrugged. "To tell you the truth, I don't know. I guess I'll just have to wait and see."

Vanessa cleared her throat. "Well, girlfriend, I guess things are looking up for both of us."

"What do you mean?"

"Kevin called me today."

Caroline's eyes widened. She put her elbows down and crossed her arms in front of her, leaning across the table.

"You let me go on and on about Derek and didn't bother to tell me about this? Is this the first time he's called since you separated?"

Vanessa shook her head. "Don't get carried away. We've spoken since he left, but only about the house or business. He still isn't saying much; he just suggested we talk about our problems."

"At least he's decided your differences are worth discussing. From what you told me, that's a big improvement."

Vanessa sighed. "Yes, it is. I guess I'm just being cautious."

Caroline nodded. "That's not a bad idea for either of us."

# Chapter Nine

The next evening Caroline examined her reflection in Vanessa's guest bedroom mirror. She had changed twice before settling on a silk three-piece outfit in a vibrant print of blues and purples. The camisole top and full skirt were topped by a matching swing jacket with elbow-length sleeves. After fastening a silver chain around her neck, she put on her silver hoop earrings. Her white clutch bag and high-heeled sandals completed the outfit.

Vanessa entered just as Caroline picked up her purse and turned to leave the room. "You look great," she said.

"Thanks."

It was a few minutes before seven when they started down the stairs together. Before they reached the bottom of the stairs, the doorbell rang.

Vanessa turned toward Caroline. "Some things never change," she said. "As I recall, Derek always was prompt."

Caroline opened the door as Vanessa reached the bottom

of the stairs. The expression in Derek's eyes when he greeted Caroline eased Vanessa's misgivings.

Caroline resisted the urge to stare at the vision before her. He was wearing tan slacks and a navy linen sport coat with a blue striped shirt. It was a perfectly ordinary outfit. So why was she so captivated by the triangle of brown skin at his open collar?

The antagonism between them had been eliminated. The wall of anger and pain had been destroyed. The door to the passion that lay behind the facade of simple courtesy was wide open and very inviting. It was up to her whether or not to walk through the portal.

Caroline glanced sharply at Derek when they entered the driveway of the same restaurant where they had had their first date. "I thought you said you weren't trying to pick up where we left off?"

Derek shook his head. "I'm not. This is where we started—sort of. I chose this restaurant because it holds some very pleasant memories for me."

He pulled into a space and stopped the car, but made no move to get out. "If you're uncomfortable with this, Caroline, we can go somewhere else."

"No, no, this is fine. It doesn't make me uncomfortable, I was just surprised."

They entered the restaurant a few minutes later. Caroline looked around her, taking in the quiet atmosphere while Derek checked on their reservation. She realized that she had no idea whether the restaurant had changed in the years since she had last been there. She had had such stars in her eyes on their first date that she had noticed few details of the decor.

Derek smiled in appreciation as she preceded him to the

table. Her loose-fitting jacket and full skirt did nothing to hide the sway of her hips. To the contrary, the soft fabric emphasized her sensual movements.

In spite of the setting, there was no discussion of the past. Caroline asked about the work that had taken him to Connecticut. She smiled when, fifteen minutes later, he was still talking.

Derek paused. "Why are you smiling?"

"Because I had forgotten what you're like when you get started on the subject of computers."

"And I'd almost forgotten what a good listener you are. You never seemed to mind when I went off on a tangent about computers, even though I think most of the time you had no idea what I was talking about."

Caroline laughed. "I still don't."

"I can't believe that. Do you own a computer?"

"In this day and age, and being a teacher, of course I have a computer. It's almost a necessity." She nodded. "So, you're right. What I said isn't entirely true. I know a little more than I did back then. Basically, I know what I need to know to do what I have to do. Fortunately, I haven't run into any problems."

He reached across the table and and took her hand in his. "If you do have any problems, you can always call me."

Heat suffused Caroline's neck and face as she met his intent gaze. It was clear that his offer was not limited to computers. She cleared her dry throat.

"You mentioned that you were in Connecticut working on a security problem with some computers. What kind of security?"

"Trying to prevent hackers from getting into the system."

"Did it work?"

Derek shrugged. "For now. The truth is that eventually

someone may find a way in. We can only hope that we're smarter than the hackers.''

"Why do they do it, anyway? The hackers, that is."

"Different reasons. Sometimes to embezzle funds or change records to their advantage. For some it's the satisfaction of knowing they broke into a supposedly secure system. Too often, though, they do it for the thrill of wreaking havoc. Before I came to Connecticut, I had to restore the nine-one-one system here in Atlanta."

"Why would someone do that? If they have some grievance against a company or agency, that's one thing, but to tamper with something like a nine-one-one system. . . ." She shook her head. "I don't know why I should be surprised. Every day some crazy person takes out their frustrations or anger on innocent people. Can't you trace the hackers?"

"It's not that easy. If they try to break in while you're on the system, you might luck out. Part of the new security installation is something that might help with that, but we can only wait and see what happens. Even if we trace one of them, there are always others to take his place."

He let go of her hand and took a sip of water. "Enough talk about computers. What about you? Is teaching all that you hoped it would be?"

She nodded. "Yes, in most ways, it is. On the other hand, there are times when it's more than I bargained for. Sometimes you have to cope with difficult students, behavior problems. It's all worthwhile, though, when you're explaining something and you look at the students and suddenly you can almost see a lightbulb go on in their heads. Then, it's wonderful."

Derek smiled. "I've heard Zoe say almost the same thing. She really loves teaching, too. That's one of the reasons she insisted on helping out at the center. Ian tried to talk her out of it. He even offered to pay someone to help with the tutoring program.''

''Why?''

''He thought it would be too much for her with the two kids. She told him she wanted to do it for herself as much as for the center.''

''And he finally accepted that?''

Derek laughed. ''If you knew Zoe better, you'd know that he didn't have much choice but to accept it.''

Caroline had learned a lot about Zoe's determination from their conversations. ''Are you saying that she's stubborn?''

Derek smiled. ''She's no more stubborn than my big brother. In fact, I think that's another thing that you and she have in common.''

Caroline raised an eyebrow. ''Are you saying that I'm stubborn?''

He cleared his throat. ''I wouldn't exactly say that either of you are stubborn. I'd say more determined than stubborn. I think that comes partly from being the youngest child in the family.''

''I see. And do you think we're all spoiled, too?''

''I said determined is a better description and of course I don't think all youngest children are spoiled. If you recall, I'm also the youngest child in my family. I just think that being the youngest child, you usually feel that you have to prove yourself.''

She smiled. ''I have a confession to make. Zoe and I actually had a discussion similar to this a few weeks ago. We were commiserating with each other about the trials involved in trying to keep older siblings from running your life. I guess after fighting all of those battles, a husband wouldn't stand a chance.''

She nodded slowly. ''I can understand Ian's concern, though. It must be hard taking care of two small children and working, even if it is part time. I'm glad I was able to help and to relieve her mind that the tutoring program wouldn't suffer. I like Zoe; she seems to be a very sweet person.''

''She is, but she can be a real pistol when the occasion calls for it.''

Caroline raised an eyebrow again. ''Oh? You sound like you've been on the receiving end of that particular trait.''

''As a matter of fact, I have. She gave me quite a little lecture the day of the barbecue. She didn't appreciate the remark I directed at you.''

Caroline looked down at her plate. ''What did you say to her?''

''Nothing. I walked away. I was angry, at first. After I cooled off, I had to admit that she was right.''

''You must have a good relationship with her. Another person might have suggested that she should mind her own business.''

''We do have a good relationship. I was there for her she and Ian first met and things weren't that great.'' He shook his head. ''But that's another story. Her anger was based mostly on the fact that I had no right to make such a remark in front of other people. She strongly suggested that any grievance I had with you should be discussed in private.''

''Did she know about us?''

''I don't think so. Ian may have mentioned that we had dated when we were in college, but that's all.''

''And that's why you decided to talk to me?''

''Not entirely. It was that and something Ian said to me.''

Caroline's eyes widened. ''Ian knew about us?''

''No, at least not until recently.'' He sighed and focused his attention on his fork, turning it over and over in his hand.

''Ian knew that I was upset, but he didn't ask any direct

questions. Zoe had told him about her lecture to me. He merely repeated her suggestion that I confront you and resolve our differences. I wasn't sure I could do that rationally and I told him so. That led to my telling him the whole story.''

Caroline took a deep breath and sipped her water slowly. She should have expected that he would tell Ian the reason for his anger. ''What did he say that made you decide to talk to me?''

''He very calmly reminded me that I was basing my assumption on a rumor. Until he said it, I hadn't seriously considered that aspect. It put everything in a whole new light and I knew that I had to hear the truth from you.''

He looked up, directly into her eyes. ''Does it upset you that I discussed it with him?''

Caroline thought about her own conversations with Vanessa. How could she be upset that he had discussed his concerns with his brother?

''No,'' she replied. ''I guess it's only normal to want to confide in someone, especially if it's a situation that disturbs you.''

Derek reached across the table and took her hand in his. ''Caroline . . .''

From the look in his eyes, she could guess what was coming and stopped him. ''Derek, if you're planning to apologize again—don't. We both decided that we should leave it alone and put it behind us. You were misled and so was I. We've pretty much exhausted the subject. I think it's past time for us to let it go.''

Derek nodded and smiled. ''Like that old saying about beating a dead horse.''

''Exactly,'' she agreed.

''Okay, I promise not to bring it up again.''

Derek directed the conversation back to her teaching

career. His questions prompted memories of some of her classroom experiences. For the next half hour, she held his attention with stories about her students.

He smiled. "I see I'm not the only one who tends to get carried away talking about work."

Caroline laughed. "From what you've said about Zoe, you should be used to it."

Until that moment, the soft music had simply lent a relaxing atmosphere to the restaurant, providing a backdrop to their conversation. She now noticed a few couples on the dance floor, and the music took on a new significance. She looked away from the dance floor to find Derek's intent gaze focused on her.

He held out his hand. "Shall we join them?"

Caroline nodded and put her hand in his. As they made their way to the dance floor, her mind was filled with memories of the past, more pleasant memories than the ones that had haunted her for the past few months. When he took her in his arms, the feelings that coursed through her were not prompted by past events.

Derek, too, was assailed by sensations that had nothing to do with memories. He pulled her close as their bodies moved in a slow rhythm to the music.

There was no more conversation; words were unnecessary. Neither of them suggested leaving the dance floor until the band announced it was taking a break. Slowly, they returned to their table. In their present mood, mundane conversation about teaching and computers was out of the question. The spell that held them in its grasp was too sweet to spoil with ordinary small talk.

When they reached their table, Derek was the first to speak. "Shall we call it a night?"

Caroline nodded and picked up her purse. Derek took her hand in his and they started toward the door.

The drive to Vanessa's house was made in companionable silence. After parking the car at the curb, Derek got out and walked around to the passenger's side. He helped her out of the car and did not let go of her hand as they walked to the front door.

Caroline unlocked the door, stepped into the foyer and turned to face him as he entered after her. "I really enjoyed myself this evening, Derek—the food, the music, everything was wonderful."

Derek smiled. "I hope the company figures in there somewhere."

"Yes, the company was a very important part of the evening."

"I'm glad to hear that because I plan for it to be the first of many such evenings." His arms encircled her as he spoke.

Caroline gazed up into his dark chocolate eyes. Recognizing the desire she had seen there many times before, she absently licked her lips.

Derek paused a moment, gauging her feelings. He lowered his head slowly, pulling her closer as his mouth met hers. His hands caressed her back, his tongue outlining the fullness of her lips, urging her to open to him.

Caroline twined her arms around his neck, surrendering to the wonderful sensations that flowed through her body. When she opened her mouth to his explorations, his questing tongue and roaming hands sent a ripple of awareness down her spine.

Derek sighed and reluctantly broke the kiss. He had promised her, and himself, that they would start over, rather than pick up where they had left off six years ago. He had not expected that one kiss would jeopardize that promise.

"I'd better be going," he murmured.

Caroline nodded.

"I'll call you tomorrow." His hand cupped her cheek,

his thumb caressing the lips he had tasted a moment earlier.
A few minutes later, he was gone.


When Caroline entered the kitchen the next morning,
Vanessa was already seated at the table. They greeted each
other as Caroline went to pour herself a mug a coffee.
Carrying it to the table, she took a seat across from her
friend.

Vanessa looked up at her. "How did it go last night?"

"It went fine," Caroline replied.

Vanessa rose and walked over to the coffeemaker. She
refilled her mug and, leaning against the counter, she turned
to face Caroline.

"I have to tell you, I was glad to hear you come in last
night. I half expected you to call and tell me that you'd see
me in the morning."

Caroline smiled. "So, mother, are you telling me that you
waited up for me?"

"No, I just happened to be awake, and I'm not trying to
play mother," she insisted, returning to her seat at the table.

"Well, you should know me better than to think I'd let
myself get that involved after one date."

"Technically, it wouldn't be after just one date. Besides,
I saw the way you two looked at each other when I surprised
you in this very kitchen."

Caroline sighed. "I won't deny that the attraction is still
there, although it took me a little by surprise. I already
admitted that to you. When he suggested dinner, we both
agreed we can't just pick up where we left off six years
ago."

"I see. Does that mean you're still not sure about him?"

"Yes and no. I'm sure that he was telling the truth about
not being engaged and, under the circumstances, his reason

for thinking I'd had an abortion were plausible. You and I agreed that Marquita was spiteful and devious and we wouldn't put anything past her.''

Vanessa nodded. "So what aren't you sure about?"

"I'm not sure about his feelings for me."

"I don't understand. You believed he was in love with you years ago. Why would you think his feelings had changed? Have yours?''

"No, as incredible as it seems, my feelings haven't changed. I was hurt and angry, but on some level I've always cared for him.''

"Cared for him? Is that your way of avoiding the 'L' word?''

"All right, I still loved him. The realization that I was still in love with him, in spite of everything, made me angry with myself. It's one of the reasons I plan to be careful about getting deeply involved.''

"Okay, you still love him. And he loved you years ago, so why do you think his feelings have changed? I realize it's been a long time, but we both agree that it's not that easy to stop loving someone.''

"It's not that I think his feelings have changed, but we're not the same people we were six years ago.''

Vanessa shook her head. "I still don't understand.''

She thought about Malcolm's attempts to persuade her to go along with whatever he planned. The ski trip had only been the final straw.

"I'm thinking about the fact that it wouldn't be the first time a man was turned off by what I consider independence.''

Vanessa laughed. "You must be kidding! Think about it, girlfriend. You haven't changed that much. You were always independent. If he fell in love with you years ago, I can't see that your independence would matter now.''

Caroline shrugged. "Maybe. I guess I'm just a little uncertain and concerned about where this is going."

"In other words, you're the one who's afraid of commitment."

"No, that's not true. I have no problem with commitment," Caroline insisted.

"Uh-huh. Then you must be looking for a guarantee. You want to be sure it will last forever."

Caroline made no reply at first. She focused her eyes on her mug. She thought about her parents' relationship, as well as the relationships of her siblings with their spouses. She had seen them together often enough to know that the touches and the looks they gave each other were no act.

"Yes, I do want to be sure it's forever," she said softly. "I don't think that's too much to expect."

Vanessa looked down at the remains of her coffee. "No, it's not too much to expect, but it's not a matter of waving a magic wand. There are no guarantees, Caroline. You have to both want it to last forever and you both have to be willing to work at it."

"I have a feeling you're not just talking about Derek and me."

"No, I'm not. I talked to Kevin again last night. He came by after you left. I don't know what's going to happen with us. He says he wants us to get back together."

"And?"

Vanessa shrugged. "And I guess, like you, I'm looking for some guarantees. I want to know that he's willing to put our relationship—to put me—first. I'm not asking him to put his career in jeopardy. I only want him to stop spending every free moment on the job."

"Did you tell him that?"

"Yes, I told him."

"What was his reaction?"

"He says he's willing to compromise."

"Doesn't the fact that he was willing to take time last night to sit down and talk tell you that he's serious?"

Vanessa nodded slowly. "You're probably right. It's not that easy, though."

"Vanessa, I'm not going to try to tell you what to do. I know how upset you were when the two of you separated, but you just finished telling me there are no guarantees. Maybe it's time for you to give him the benefit of the doubt."

Vanessa tilted her head to the side. "You know, that's one of the things that I like about our friendship. We don't try to run each other's lives, but we don't have to tiptoe around each other and worry about whether or not to voice our opinions."

"Does that mean you'll think about giving Kevin a chance?"

"Yes, I'll think about it. I guess if you can give Derek the benefit of the doubt after what you've been through, the least I can do is give Kevin the same."

Caroline held up her mug and smiled. "Here's to us."

Vanessa returned the salute. "And to true friendship."

# Chapter Ten

On the following Friday, Derek took Caroline to dinner at the Sundial Restaurant, high atop the Westin Peachtree Plaza Hotel. As the restaurant slowly revolved, the view of Atlanta from that vantage point was spectacular.

"Our reservation is for eight, so we're a little early. I thought you might like to take a look through the telescopes and peruse the history wall first," he explained.

Caroline was glad he had planned that part of the evening before dinner. Once they were seated, she had difficulty keeping her eyes off of him.

Her insistence to Vanessa that she planned to proceed slowly with their relationship was being put to the test. She had to be sure of his feelings, but every time their gazes met, which was often, she felt a strong tug at her emotions. It would be very easy to throw caution to the wind.

Derek had his own problems concentrating on such ordinary matters as menus. His gaze strayed often to his companion. The black low-cut dress revealed just a hint of cleavage, but it was enough to remind him of what lay beneath the fabric. He was amazed that images from the past could be so easily conjured up. He remembered the feel of her soft, silky skin beneath his fingers.

When the waiter approached to fill their water glasses, they turned their attention to a more serious perusal of the menu. Conversation for most of the remainder of the evening was limited to such ordinary topics as music and books. Caroline commented on the sights she had seen and the changes that had taken place in the city since she had attended school there.

They lingered over dinner and coffee until Derek proposed a visit to a small jazz club. He was not so much interested in listening to music as he was in prolonging the evening.

A few hours later, they decided to call it a night. During the drive to Vanessa's house, they made a date to visit the Atlanta Botanical Gardens the next day.

"As long as it's not a trip that has to start early in the morning," Caroline said. "I don't think I could do it justice with one eye closed."

Derek smiled. "I promise it won't be before noon. Is that good enough?"

"I should be fully awake by then," she agreed.

All too soon, Derek was depositing her at Vanessa's door. He would much rather have been ushering her into his own home, but they needed more time before taking that step in their relationship.

Caroline unlocked the door, stepped into the foyer, and turned to face him. "I don't think I have to tell you that I had a wonderful time this evening."

"I'm glad," he murmured, taking her in his arms. "But the evening's not quite over yet."

Caroline's arms encircled his neck. "No?"

"No," he replied, just before his lips captured hers. Unlike their previous kiss, there was no hesitation. His mouth moved slowly over hers before his tongue slipped between her lips to play tag with hers. His hands stroked her back, coming to rest on the curve of her hips.

Caroline's fingers caressed the nape of his neck. The smell of his cologne mingled with his own scent as he pulled her closer. Engulfed in an aura of desire, she could have easily discarded her resolve to be sure of the depth of his feelings before becoming intimately involved.

When he finally broke the kiss, she could not decide if she was glad or sorry that they were standing in Vanessa's foyer. Had they been in more private surroundings, her resolve might have easily gone down the drain.

"I'd better leave now, before I forget where we are," he murmured, echoing her thoughts.

Caroline nodded. "I'll see you tomorrow."

After one last brief kiss on her cheek, he turned and left. Caroline closed and locked the door behind him. She leaned against it for a moment, letting out a long breath. Then she started up the stairs to bed.


After that second date, Caroline had dinner with Derek at least twice a week. They were together every weekend, taking trips to various museums and parks. They rediscovered all of the facets of each other's personalities that had first drawn them together years ago. They also discovered that those basic traits had not changed.

For the most part, just being together was sufficiently satisfying. They had agreed not to rush into an intimate relationship, but it had become evident that friendly companionship was not enough. Each time they went out, he deposited her on Vanessa's doorstep with a hot, lingering kiss, but suggested nothing more.

The summer was passing much too quickly for Caroline. She wanted him, but she was still uncertain that she was ready to take the next step. As she had told Malcolm, intimacy was a big deal to her.

She had never been able to separate "making love" from "being in love." She was in love with Derek. Although he had never actually said the words, she believed he was in love with her. Maybe she was being overly cautious. If only she had more time.

Angela was unaware that Derek and Caroline were dating, but she had noticed a change in her newest volunteer. She still avoided making any references to Derek, although Caroline no longer tensed when one of the other employees mentioned him.

The last week before the center was due to close for the summer, Angela met with Caroline. "I've already told you about the closing program for the students, but I wanted to meet with you alone. I just want to thank you, again, for your help this summer."

"I've enjoyed it, Angela. It's great to see the progress some of the students have made with just a little more attention. It's not the same as one-on-one tutoring, but I think it makes a big difference."

"The real proof will be in their grades when they return to school next month. Our after-school program isn't as intense as the summer tutoring, but it helps to keep them on track."

"Speaking of the after-school program, will Zoe continue with that?"

Angela nodded. "Right now, yes. She's made some changes, though. She's cutting back to three days a week and she'll bring Savannah with her."

"Do you think that'll work out?"

"I think so. We both agreed to give it a try. It's only for a couple of hours, so hopefully Savannah won't have time to get restless."

Caroline smiled. "She seems to be quite an active child."

"That she is, but she's basically well-behaved. I don't envision any major problems."

"By the way," Caroline said, changing the subject, "I think the idea of having a recognition program is great. I try to give the students as much encouragement as possible, but actually receiving a certificate to acknowledge their improvement means a lot to them."

"That's why we manage to give a certificate to each of them. We can always find some facet of growth to emphasize."

The students were not the only object of Angela's attention at the center's closing program. It became clear to her that Caroline and Derek had overcome their differences. In fact, the looks they exchanged indicated more than a simple truce.

Caroline felt a few moments of anticipation when Derek invited her to his home for lunch the day after the closing of the center. She arrived shortly after eleven-thirty and parked in the wide driveway. Her hand was poised to ring the bell when Derek opened it.

His gaze scanned her appearance for a few seconds before ushering her into the foyer. She had chosen to wear a straight cut sundress of pale yellow linen. When she moved past him, he caught a glimpse of leg exposed by the side slit.

She had only taken a few steps when he gently pulled her into his arms.

"Welcome to my home," he murmured, seconds before claiming her lips.

Before her arrival, Caroline expected he would offer to show her the house. After the kiss, she wondered if it would be wise to tour the house. Such a tour could possibly end abruptly in his bedroom.

As if he had read her thoughts, Derek took her hand and asked, "Would you like to see the rest of the house?"

"I'd love to," she replied, ignoring the questionable wisdom of that move.

He led her through the hallway. Its ivory wallpaper with pinstripes of hunter green, gold, and burgundy coordinated with the oriental runner on the hardwood floor. Floor-to-ceiling square fluted columns on either side separated the hallway from the living room. The hunter green walls of the living room were offset by pale golden oak woodwork that matched the columns at the entryway.

Along the wall to their right was an oversized, overstuffed sofa in a fabric with stripes of varying widths of hunter green, gold, and burgundy. A large square mahogany coffeetable separated the sofa from the oversized chair and ottoman that were covered in a predominantly green, modified paisley print. An entertainment center and bookcases filled most of the wall directly opposite the sofa.

A green-veined ivory marble fireplace on the wall to the right of the sofa was framed in the same golden oak and flanked by two windows that extended almost floor to ceiling. Tailored balloon shades in the same stripe as the sofa hung at the windows topped by cornices that matched the fabric on the chair and ottoman.

The off-white carpet underfoot had a just a hint of gold in its hue and matched the color of the ceiling overhead.

The skylights in the sloped ceiling kept the room bright in spite of the dark walls.

"It's beautiful, Derek."

"Thanks. I have to confess that I had a little help from a professional decorator, but the colors were my idea."

They continued their tour past another set of columns to the dining room. The same colors were echoed in the walls and woodwork as in the living room. The parson chairs at the mahogany table were upholstered in the same print as the chairs in the living room. A matching mahogany breakfront extended the length opposite two more tall windows that were separated by the mahogany server.

Their next stop was the kitchen. The cabinets were finished in the same golden oak she had seen in the other rooms. Thanks to a wide bank of windows on one wall, this room was also light and airy, in spite of the dark green marble-like counters and hunter green walls. One counter was extended to form a small breakfast nook.

"This is quite a kitchen for a bachelor," Caroline commented. "I thought most bachelors lived on take-out food."

"Not this one. At one time in my life that was true, but after a while you get tired of restaurants and take-out. In the past few years I've learned to appreciate my mother's insistence that her sons learn to cook nutritious meals."

"Well, something smells good, so I guess I'll appreciate her foresight before the day is over."

"I hope so. For now, shall we finish our tour?"

Caroline nodded and they returned to the foyer and proceeded up the stairs. One of the bedrooms was furnished as an office and another was done traditionally in shades of blue and green.

More thought had gone into the decor of the master bedroom. The walls were painted in cinnabar red, the perfect backdrop to the solid black headboard and the black, gray, and white print of the bedspread and tailored drapes. Black furniture and accents of red and shades of gray and white completed the picture.

Caroline took a deep breath as she looked around. The ambience of the room was about as sensual as she could ever imagine, or maybe it was the fact that Derek was just inches away from her.

He led her through to the master bath, which repeated the same cinnabar-red walls. The focal point of the room was the square gray marble enclosure for the large whirlpool tub. A tall black chest matched the long vanity topped by a gray marble counter and sink. White accents and white fluffy towels in a black cabinet beside the tub added the final touch.

Caroline was envisioning the two of them in that huge tub when Derek's words broke the spell. "Well, that's it."

He glanced at his watch. Then he took her elbow and ushered her toward the door. "I think lunch is ready by now."

The rest of the afternoon passed pleasantly. They ate lunch at the breakfast counter in the kitchen after they agreed that the dining room was too formal a setting.

They were halfway through their meal when Derek broached the subject of her impending return to Connecticut. "Now that your tutoring responsibilities have ended, will you be returning to Connecticut next week?"

Caroline shook her head. "No, I still have more than two weeks before school starts. I thought I'd use the time here to do a little more traveling. I've never been to Savannah. I'll probably drive down and spend a few days there."

"I have a better idea. Have you been to Charleston?"

"No."

"How do you feel about my driving to Savannah with

you? We could spend a few days there, and then we could cruise up to Charleston and look around.''

"I didn't know there were cruises like that. Do you have to take a tour as part of the package, or what?''

Derek smiled. "It's not a tour at all. I'm suggesting that we cruise to Charleston on my boat.''

Caroline raised an eyebrow. "Your boat?''

He nodded. "I have a forty-five foot cruiser. It's docked at a marina near Savannah.''

Caroline hesitated. What he suggested sounded like a very intimate setting. She loved him and she wanted him. For a brief moment, Malcolm's planned weekend came to mind. This was very different, though. Derek had made no underhanded plan without her knowledge. Having her there in his home gave him the perfect opportunity to attempt to seduce her, but he had made no move to do so. The only question was whether she was ready for this step in their relationship.

Derek misunderstood her hesitancy. "I promise you, it's perfectly safe. You don't get seasick, do you?''

She shook her head. "I've never been on a boat for any length of time, but I don't think I'd have a problem. I've never suffered any other motion sickness. I suppose I could always have medicine on hand, just in case.''

He took her hand, nodding slowly as he considered the other possible reason for her uncertainty. "If it's not seasickness, there's only one other thing I can think of that has you concerned. I promise you that I have no ulterior motive.

"I've made no secret of the fact that I want you. Wanting to make love to you is a natural part of my feelings for you. You have to believe, though, that it wouldn't mean anything unless you want it, too.''

"I just don't think I'm ready for that step.''

"I'd never try to coerce you into a situation that would make you uncomfortable, Caroline. The boat has two separate cabins, as well as other sleeping berths. You can have your choice. With or without having you in my bed, I want us to share the time you have left before you return to Connecticut.''

Caroline nodded. ''You're absolutely sure this boat is safe?''

Derek laughed at the sudden change in the subject of her concern. ''I'm absolutely sure.''

The rest of the afternoon was spent making plans for the trip. They decided to leave for Savannah early Monday morning, giving them time to settle on the boat and see a little of the city.

''Of course, that's provided I can get away from the job. I'll talk to Ian this afternoon. If there's a problem, I'll let you know this evening.''

After Caroline left to go home and dress for dinner, Derek called his brother. ''I wanted to check with you to see if there's any reason I can't take a couple of weeks' vacation.''

''None that I can think of, Derek. This is a little sudden, though. Are you okay?''

''Actually, Ian, I haven't felt this good in quite some time. I'm planning a trip to Savannah and Charleston with Caroline.''

''Caroline? It sounds like you've been holding out on me. When did this come about?''

''We've been dating for a few weeks.''

''So you have been holding out on me. I guess you two have ironed out your differences if you've been seeing each other for a few weeks. Especially if you're planning a vacation together.''

"Yes, we ironed out our differences. I won't go into any detail. I'll just say that you'd have every right to say 'I told you so.' "

"I'm happy for you, Derek. Take your vacation and have a good time."

"Thanks, Ian."

# Chapter Eleven

The next morning, Caroline informed Vanessa of her plans for the following week. "I feel a little guilty. I know you had already said you couldn't take off to come to Savannah with me, but when I mentioned it before, I had only planned to be gone for a few days."

Vanessa cocked her head to one side. "You've been here most of the summer, Caroline. It's not like we haven't had time together. Besides, far be it for me to interfere with a romantic tryst, on a secluded boat, no less."

"It's not a romantic tryst, Vanessa. It's a sightseeing trip, that's all."

Vanessa laughed. "Right, whatever you say."

On Monday morning, Caroline was up bright and early. Vanessa was having her morning coffee when Caroline joined her in the kitchen.

"Good morning," Vanessa greeted her, grinning. "You're up awfully early. I guess you're really looking forward to this trip. I wonder why."

"Don't start, Vanessa," Caroline said, helping herself to coffee. "We want to get an early start. I think it's about a four-hour drive to Savannah."

Vanessa rose from her seat and carried her mug to the sink. After pouring the remainder of her coffee down the drain, she turned to Caroline.

Hugging her friend, she murmured, "Don't mind me. I told you before, I think it's great that you two have finally gotten back together. Have a good time."

"Thanks. I'm sure I will, whatever happens."

Vanessa could not resist a parting comment. "By the way, what shall I tell your mother if she happens to call? I mean, I can tell her you took a side trip to Savannah, but what if she asks for the telephone number for your hotel?"

Caroline rolled her eyes. "She has my cell phone number and I'm sure you'll think of an acceptable explanation. Good-bye, Vanessa."

Vanessa laughed and left the kitchen. The doorbell rang just as she reached the front door. She opened it to Derek.

"Good morning. Caroline's in the kitchen and I'm on my way to work." As Derek headed toward the kitchen, Vanessa called out, "Have a good time."

Caroline was seated at the table when Derek greeted her. He planted a kiss on her temple and sat down across from her.

"Have you had breakfast?"

"Just coffee. I don't usually eat breakfast."

He shook his head. "That's a bad habit."

"Yes, I know. My mother has been telling me for years that breakfast is the most important meal of the day. When I'm working, there never seems to be enough time, though."

"So what's your excuse today?"

She shrugged. "I didn't want to keep you waiting."

Derek laughed. "Oh, so you plan to blame it on me. In that case, let's get started. We can stop for breakfast on our way to Savannah. Speaking of your mother, I'd better give you my cell phone number in case she calls."

Caroline shook her head. "That's okay. I have mine with me, and she and Vanessa have that number."

He stood up. "In that case, I guess we're ready to go."

Within minutes, he had stowed her bag in the trunk and they were on the road. After nearly two hours on the road, Derek exited the highway.

"I think we'd better stop and let you get something to eat. I wouldn't want to have you fainting from hunger before we reach Savannah." He smiled and added, "I'm not sure I'm up to carrying you aboard the boat."

Caroline punched his shoulder playfully. "Are you hinting that I've gained weight since college?"

He glanced at her. "I'd say a little. Mind you, I'm not complaining. From what I've seen, you gained it in all the right places."

The heat crept slowly up Caroline's neck. Just as she had known him intimately, he, too, was more intimately acquainted with her than any man she had ever known. The heat spread through her body at his next comment.

"Speaking of gaining weight in all the right places, you did bring a bathing suit didn't you?"

Caroline cleared her throat. "Yes, I brought a bathing suit."

"Of course, if we find a secluded beach, you really won't need the bathing suit."

"Secluded or not, Derek, I'll need the suit."

Derek heaved an exaggerated sigh. "Oh well, it was just a thought. You can't blame me for trying."

*      *      *

By midafternoon they had arrived at the marina. Derek parked the car and retrieved their bags from the trunk. He then led the way to the dock.

Caroline took a deep breath when he led her to the imposing vessel moored alongside other boats, some larger and some smaller. Her knowledge of boats was very limited, but she was impressed.

Derek boarded first. He set their bags on the deck and held out a hand to help her aboard. After a short tour of the cockpit, he picked up their bags and led the way to the salon.

It was furnished like a normal living room except that the furniture was bolted to the floor. A round coffeetable in teak separated two navy blue chairs from the navy blue, rust, and tan plaid banquette in front of the window.

The dining area behind one side of the banquette had swivel chairs upholstered in the same plaid as the sofa. Navy blue drapes, tan carpeting, and rust accents gave the salon the finishing touches.

Caroline only had time for a cursory examination before Derek urged her below. They descended a few steps to a long hallway. He set their bags on the floor midway down the hall.

"This is the master cabin," he informed her, opening the door at the end of the hallway. The queen-size bed was enclosed in teak paneling that matched the wall of built-in cabinets. The royal blue-and-white print bed cover and drapes were offset by the white carpeting and accents.

Taking her elbow, he directed her back toward the stairs. He stopped near the spot where he had set their bags and opened the door to a smaller cabin with a full-size bed, also enclosed in teak. It was decorated in varying shades of blue and green with yellow accents.

"You can have your choice."

"The smaller cabin is fine," she assured him.

He nodded, picked up her bag from the hall and set it inside the cabin. "I'll leave you to unpack. Afterward, if you'd like, we can take a drive around Savannah."

"That sounds fine."

Caroline took little time unpacking and they were soon on their way. Derek gave her an abbreviated tour of the city and its historic squares, one of the most fascinating aspects of the city. It was early evening when they completed their tour.

"We might as well have dinner before we head back to the boat," he suggested.

They stopped at a small restaurant on River Street. After a leisurely dinner, they rambled through the shops lining the cobblestone street. As they strolled Riverfront Plaza, Caroline stifled a yawn.

Derek chuckled. "I guess I coerced you into getting up a little too early this morning. Shall we head back to the boat?"

"Sorry. I think that's a good idea."


After touring the Savannah History Museum the next day, they drove through town again, stopping at the First African Baptist Church. "Have you been here before?" she asked, scanning the brochure.

"If you knew my parents better, you wouldn't have to ask that question. When we were kids, we spent most of the summer being shuffled from one historic sight to the other."

Caroline read the brochure aloud. "According to this, the

church was founded in 1773. It's believed to be the oldest continuously active African-American Baptist congregation in North America." She looked up from the printed page. "It's amazing that it was formed and it survived in spite of slavery."

When they left the church, they toured a few of the squares that they had missed the previous day. Then Derek drove to Tybee Island, where they visited the lighthouse.

As they looked out over the channel, Caroline commented, "It's a good thing I'm not afraid of heights. You seem to have a penchant for tall buildings and structures."

Derek smiled. "I hadn't really thought about it, but you do have a point."

A few minutes later, they descended the stairs. When they reached the car, Derek suggested a stroll on the beach.

"Good idea," she agreed, slipping out of her sandals. "It's not often I get an opportunity to wiggle my toes in the sand."

An hour later later, they returned to the car. "Are you ready for dinner?"

"Do we need to go back to the boat and change clothes first?"

Derek shook his head. "I'm sure we can find a restaurant that will let us in dressed as we are." He looked down at her feet. "I think you'll have to put your shoes on, though."

She held onto his arm to steady herself while she brushed off her feet and slipped them into her sandals. He then held the door open while she settled herself in the passenger's seat.

"Tomorrow we'll head up to Charleston. We've seen a few of the more interesting parts of Savannah. If we have time when we come back to Savannah, we can take in a few more of the sights here."

\* \* \*

Caroline awakened the next morning to the smell of coffee brewing. She donned her robe and followed the aroma to the galley on the far side of the dining area. Derek was seated at the dining area table, coffee mug in one hand and protractor in the other. Spread out in front of him was a large chart.

"Good morning," she greeted him.

"Morning," he murmured, not looking up, preoccupied with the papers on the table.

After helping herself to coffee, she sat down across from him. Taking a sip of her coffee, she asked, "What's that? A map?"

He finally looked up. "Sort of. It's called a chart. Basically it's a map of the ocean, showing the channels and the depth of the water at any given point. You have to navigate through the channels."

Caroline frowned. "It sounds complicated. Have you done this before without any help? I mean, don't you need a crew or something? This is a pretty big boat."

Derek smiled. "You're not chickening out on me, are you? I've taken a very comprehensive boating course, and, yes, I've done this on my own a number of times. In fact, Ian and I have piloted his sixty-foot yacht to the Bahamas a few times, just the two of us. This boat's a lot smaller and I promise you, you'll be perfectly safe with me."

He took her hand and looked at her more closely. "You're not really afraid, are you? I wouldn't do anything to put you in danger, Caroline."

"I know that. I'm not really afraid, just a little nervous. I've only been on a boat one other time in my life and I don't think the ferry to Staten Island counts."

Derek chuckled. "No, I don't think that counts."

"How soon will we be leaving?"

He looked at his watch. "About half an hour. If you hurry and get dressed, you can sit in the cockpit with me. You'll see how safe it is and get the full effect as we head out into the channel."

Half an hour later, dressed in white shorts and a bright red-and-yellow print blouse, Caroline joined him in the cockpit. Rather than her usual sandals, she wore the white canvas deck shoes Derek had suggested. She had a moment of apprehension when he pointed out the storage area for the life jackets.

"It's a precaution, Caroline. Everyone on board should be aware of the location and proper use of the life jackets." He indicated the seat next to the pilot's chair. "Have a seat. I'll just be a minute."

He left her to release the ropes mooring the boat to the dock. A moment later, he rejoined her, started the motor, and steered the boat into the channel.

As they cruised up the coastline, Derek pointed out Hilton Head Island and some of the smaller sea islands. After a few minutes, Caroline relaxed and enjoyed the scenery and the short voyage.

# Chapter Twelve

They were docked in Charleston before noon. He turned to face her after he had maneuvered the vessel into the slip and turned off the motor.

"That wasn't so bad, was it?"

"It was wonderful. I never realized cruising could give you such a great feeling of freedom. Being out there on the water is so peaceful."

A moment later, she joined him on deck as he secured the lines. "A thought just occurred to me. How are we going to get around here in Charleston? Your car's in Savannah."

After completing his task, he replied, "I called ahead to rent a car." He urged her inside to the salon. "I just have to call and let them know we've arrived. They'll deliver it to us here at the marina."

"At the risk of giving you a big head, I have to admit I'm impressed. You handled the boat so well I forgot I was nervous, and you seem to have thought of everything."

His arms encircled her waist. Nuzzling her neck, he whispered, "I tried. Unfortunately, some things are beyond my control."

At that moment, Caroline was not so sure that that was true. Her own control over her emotions was nonexistent and her control over her actions was being held by a slender thread. She cleared her throat and gently pulled away from him.

He loosened his hold and let her go after planting a brief kiss on her surprised lips. "I'll call the car rental company. We should have time for a trip to the open-air market."

"What's that?"

"It's rather like a flea market. You'll find some beautiful arts and crafts handiwork: carved wood, sweet grass baskets, dried flowers, and arrangements. You'll see for yourself."

That afternoon, she did see for herself. After lunch they strolled through the market. Caroline was especially taken with the sweet grass baskets. Not only were they beautiful examples of craftsmanship, but their tantalizing fragrance set them apart from any basket she had ever seen.

One particular set caught Caroline's eye: three baskets in graduated sizes that fit inside each other. She had already purchased several items; gifts for her family and Vanessa. Now she balked at the price the vendor was asking.

Derek watched as she examined several other baskets, but it was obvious to him that she really wanted the set. He offered to purchase it for her.

"No, Derek. I can't let you do that."

"Why not?"

She hesitated, trying to think of the right words. "I just can't. It's too much."

"Caroline, let me ask you a question. If Vanessa offered them to you as a gift, would you accept them?"

"That's different."

"Why?"

Caroline sighed. "Why are you giving me such a hard time about this?"

Derek smiled. "You're the one who's giving me a hard time. I just want to buy you a gift as a memento of this trip. Why won't you let me have that pleasure?"

"All right, Derek."

He paid the woman who had been listening to their exchange with a broad smile. She wrapped the baskets and handed them to Caroline.

Caroline turned to Derek. "Thank you."

"You're welcome," he replied, taking the package from her. "I'll carry it. Those baskets can be heavy."

They continued their tour of the market. It was early evening before they decided they had had enough.

"Do you want to have dinner before we return to the boat or shall we stop and get take-out?"

"Take-out sounds good. I can kick off my shoes and we can eat it in relaxed comfort on board."

Derek smiled and glanced down at her sandal-clad feet. "You should have worn sneakers. They're much better for all this walking."

Caroline looked down at her green-and-yellow sundress. She had changed clothes while they waited for the car to be delivered.

"They wouldn't have been very fashionable with this outfit, though."

Derek clasped her elbow and steered her toward the parking lot. "Okay, take-out it is."

* * *

As they sat across from each other in the comfort of the boat's salon, Caroline again questioned the wisdom of her decision to make this trip with him. Staring into his chestnut-colored eyes as he fed her tidbits of shrimp from his plate created an intimacy she had not experienced in years.

When she absently licked the barbecue sauce from her fingers, he stopped her. The heat suffused her neck and her gaze never left his as his tongue began disposing of the sauce. A tingling sensation traveled through her hand and up her arm as his mouth engulfed her fingers, his tongue swirling around them.

With some effort, Caroline looked away from his mesmerizing gaze and tugged gently to loosen her hand from his grasp. She cleared her throat.

"What plans do you have for us tomorrow? Anything special?"

Derek did not answer immediately. He had promised himself he would not try to rush her into a physical relationship. He had to leave that decision up to her.

"I have a few possibilities in mind. We can decide in the morning."


The next day they drove to St. Helena Island to visit the Penn Center. Derek smiled when she read the brochure aloud.

"The center was originally founded by Quakers as a school to educate the newly freed slaves. The small museum contains artifacts showing the history of the Sea Islands and its ties to West Africa. One of its main goals is the preservation of the Gullah culture, a blend of African crafts, tradition, and language."

When she looked up and saw his smile, she bit her lip. "I did it again, didn't I? I keep acting as if this is your first trip here, or even worse, like you can't read the brochure for yourself. I can't help it. It's all new and exciting to me. I guess I get carried away."

Derek chuckled. "I don't mind. I don't understand, though. You live in Conneticut and New England is full of historical sites."

Caroline shook her head. "Not like this. There are some sites that are pertinent to African-American history, but nothing that compares to this."

When they returned to Charleston, Derek drove to Battery Park. They strolled through the park for a while before taking a seat on one of the benches to watch the boats sailing back and forth on the water. Afterward, they toured the historic section of the city.

Before having dinner, they returned to the boat to change clothes. Derek had made reservations at a small restaurant just outside of Charleston. In addition to the exceptional food, it offered live music for dancing.

Caroline gave a great deal of consideration to her outfit for the evening. She finally chose a loose-fitting chemise-style dress with spaghetti straps in a muted floral-print georgette fabric with an ivory background. The matching duster would provide some protection against the chill of air-conditioning, if necessary.

Later that evening, Caroline knew she had only been kidding herself to think she would need a wrap to keep her warm. She had removed the duster soon after their arrival and it remained draped over the chair. Each time she looked into the eyes of the man sitting across the table, it seemed the temperature in the room went up a few degrees. When he took her in his arms on the dance floor, the figure tripled.

After a while, she relaxed and closed her eyes. A sigh of contentment escaped her lips and she let the sweet sensations wash over her.

As they moved in a slow rhythm to the sultry music, Derek's hand caressed the smooth, silky skin exposed by the low-cut back of her dress. When she raised her head and gazed into his eyes, he tightened his arms around her, pulling her closer.

An hour later, Derek suggested they call it a night. They returned briefly to their table. Caroline draped her duster over her arm and they started toward the door.

Preoccupied with the emotions churning inside of them, the drive to the marina was made in near silence. Derek parked the car and they walked hand in hand to the boat.

Caroline frowned slightly in disappointment when Derek deposited her at the doorway of her cabin with only a brief kiss. His lips had barely touched hers when he pulled away. What had she expected? He had made it clear that the first move was hers.

"Good night, Caroline."

"Good night," she murmured, before entering the room and closing the door behind her.

Her expression had not escaped Derek's notice. An evening of holding her tempting form in his arms, surrounded by the enticing fragrance of her perfume and her own sweet essence had prompted concern for his own self-control. He questioned his ability to live up to his vow not to apply some gentle persuasion to get her into his bed.

In his mind, she was already there. Visions of her filled his dreams. Every time he looked at her, he wanted to touch her and every time he touched her, he wanted more.

* * *

Caroline awakened just before dawn. She had slept fitfully, thanks to dreams of Derek and her own indecision. She lay there, trying to clear her mind of disturbing images, but it was no use. The thoughts churning in her mind made sleep impossible. She finally gave up, put on her robe over her pajamas, and went up on deck.

She watched as the sun spread its amber glow across the indigo sky, lightening it first to turquoise and then to a clear wedgwood blue. Just as the sun cleared the horizon, Derek appeared, clad only in his pajama pants. Caroline turned her attention from the spectacle in the sky to the much more interesting spectacle beside her.

She swallowed hard as her gaze took in the broad expanse of chocolate-colored skin with its sprinkling of hairs. Her survey unconsciously followed the path of the narrow pelt that tapered down his abdomen to disappear beneath the waistband of his pajamas.

"What's wrong? Are you okay?" He asked, sitting down beside her on the cushioned deck seat.

Caroline stared at him for a second as he approached, before recovering her voice. "I'm fine. I woke up and couldn't get back to sleep, so I thought I'd come up here and watch the sunrise."

She looked up at the sky, now a pale blue with just a hint of gold. "I don't get this chance often. Even when I'm up early enough to see it, the scenery is nothing like this."

Derek nodded. "It gives you a different perspective, doesn't it?"

She shifted in her seat to face him, expecting his attention to be focused on the sky. Instead, it was focused on her, and she met his intent gaze. Her voice came out as barely a whisper.

"Yes, it does."

A few seconds later, she was in his arms. Their lips met as if drawn together by a magnet. The result was more like a match to dry kindling.

Derek's mouth slanted across hers, hungrily devouring all she offered. It was not enough. His hand slid through the opening of her robe and under the shirt of her pajamas, to capture her full round breast, kneading it until his thumb grazed its rigid nipple.

Caroline moaned and clutched his shoulders before splaying her hands across his back. When her exploring fingers slid beneath the waistband of his pajamas, it was Derek's turn to moan.

His lips left hers to trail kisses down her neck. Pushing aside her robe, he continued across her collarbone and down between her breasts.

When his tongue replaced his fingers at her breast, Caroline gasped. "I think I lied, Derek."

Her meaning did not sink in at first. "Lied about what, baby?" he murmured, before resuming his activity.

"About not being ready for the next step," she whispered.

Her words captured his full attention. He raised his head and looked into her eyes, now glazed with desire. "Are you sure?" he asked, against his better judgment.

She nodded. "Very sure."

He stood and urged her to her feet, before lifting her in his arms and starting toward the cabin. When he reached the bottom of the stairs, he went straight to his own cabin.

"I thought you didn't have the strength to carry me?" she asked, smiling.

"It's amazing what the proper incentive will do," he replied, setting her on her feet.

He immediately disposed of the robe, which now hung open, exposing her short pajamas. Grasping the hem of her shirt, he quickly pulled it up over her head and tossed it aside.

Before she could accustom herself to this change, he slid his fingers into the waistband of her shorts. Kneeling in front of her, he slowly eased them down her legs. His fingers tantalized her hips and derriere and his warm breath wreaked havoc with her senses. She clutched his shoulders, in serious danger of collapsing in a heap.

Her pulse rate tripled when he stood and loosened the drawstring of his pajamas, allowing them to slide down his legs and pool at his feet. She opened her mouth, but no words would come out. All she could do was stare at the visible evidence of his desire.

He took a step forward and she looked up to see the passion burning in his eyes. She moaned again, deep in her throat, at the first contact of skin to skin. He wrapped his arms around her, lifting her slightly off her feet. His manhood pressed gently against the triangle of hair at the juncture of her thighs.

Derek carried her to the bed and laid her on the cool sheets. A moment later, he lay down beside her and resumed his slow, thorough exploration. His tongue drew circles on her breasts while his hands roamed over her body.

"You taste so good," he murmured against her skin. Her intoxicating fragrance enveloped him.

Caroline was busy making discoveries of her own as her fingers caressed the flexing muscles of his back, before moving to his chest to play in the sprinkling of hairs. Her hand moved lower to explore the thicker mat of hair and the rigid shaft in its midst. Her fingers caressed its smooth, taut skin just as his own hand reached the silky pelt between her thighs.

Caroline's senses were overwhelmed by the enticing scent of his cologne and the pleasure he aroused with his hands and mouth. Her own explorations ceased and she moaned his name when he insinuated his fingers into the secret place hidden by the triangle of curls and began slowly stroking the moist nub.

"Please, Derek," she pleaded breathlessly when he left her to retrieve the small foil packet from the nightstand.

"Baby, I plan to do just that," he promised.

Moments later, he was settled between her soft thighs. His lips captured hers as he entered her hot, wet sheath. His tongue mimicked the motions of his lower body as they luxuriated in the sensations that carried them closer and closer to ecstasy.

Caroline felt as if she would burst from sheer pleasure. She wrapped her legs around his waist, drawing him deeper and deeper into her until she cried out his name in climax.

Derek's release followed immediately, her body contracting in spasms of pleasure and driving him over the edge. He collapsed in total contentment. Moments later, they drifted off to sleep in each other's arms.

# Chapter Thirteen

The sun had risen high in the sky when its rays peeked through the curtains of the cabin's porthole, waking Caroline for the second time that morning. She stirred and rolled over. The minor twinge of pain caused by her slight movement reminded her of the recent activities she and Derek had shared.

She sat up in bed, looking around the cabin. Derek was nowhere in sight, but she spied her pajamas and robe on a chair across the room. Throwing back the covers, she swung her feet around to the side of the bed. She had one foot on the floor when Derek entered. Automatically pulling the covers over her nude body, she slid back into bed.

Derek chuckled. "I don't believe what I just saw."

"What do you mean?"

"You, covering yourself. Don't you think it's a little late to be hiding all those beautiful curves?"

Caroline looked away from his gaze, absently pleating

the sheet. She cleared her throat. "I wasn't hiding. It was just a reflex action."

He leaned over and kissed her cheek. Her pulse quickened at the closeness of his bare chest and the spicy fresh scent emanating from him.

"In that case," he whispered in her ear, "why don't you get out of that bed and get your robe so we can have breakfast?"

Caroline turned her head slightly and looked up, directly into his eyes. What she saw there gave her the reassurance she suddenly realized she had been seeking.

"Is that a dare?"

Derek returned her smile. "Not really. It's more like a fervent request."

"In that case, how could I refuse?" She threw back the covers in one quick movement and swung her feet over the side of the bed for the second time that morning.

Derek took a deep breath as she rose and strolled over to the chair. When she picked up the robe, he was tempted to snatch it from her hands. The muscles in his abdomen tightened when she turned to face him before slowly slipping her arms into the sleeves and pulling it closed.

His gaze never left hers as he slowly closed the short distance between them. He planted a brief kiss on her lips and murmured, "I think I just discovered that you have a slight wanton streak."

Caroline laughed. "You started it."

He nodded. "Guilty as charged, and after breakfast, I plan to finish it." He took her hand and led her out of the cabin. "But first, I think I'd better feed you. You'll need your nourishment."

Caroline remembered those words later that afternoon, lying in his arms. She had silently and jokingly questioned whether she should consider his words a threat or a promise. Whichever they had been, he had lived up to it.

There was no sightseeing in the city that day. After cruising around the outlying sea islands, they spent the remainder of the afternoon reclining on the deck, hand in hand. They watched contentedly as the sun set, casting a brilliant crimson and gold glow and painting the sky as it darkened to muted stripes of sapphire and amethyst.

The ball of fire had just disappeared below the horizon when Derek asked, "What would you like for dinner? There are steaks in the freezer, or we can go out."

Caroline was still clad in her bathing suit from her afternoon of sunbathing. Her only concession had been to don a sarong after a few hours.

"I think I'd rather stay here. That way I won't have to get dressed. I need to shower first, though. I'm starting to feel sticky from the suntan lotion."

Derek stood up. Grinning, he urged her to her feet. "Putting it that way, staying in certainly has my vote. The shower sounds like a good idea, too. Maybe I'll join you."

Caroline had starting walking toward the cabin. She stopped and glanced at him over her shoulder.

"I don't think that's a good idea. If we're planning to eat anytime in the next two hours, I think you'd better use your shower and I'll use the one in the hallway."

"You mean I can't interest you in an appetizer before dinner?" he suggested, wrapping his arms around her. His hand caressed the enticing curve of her derriere.

She placed her palms against his bare chest, gently running her fingers through the sprinkling of hairs. "The problem is that your appetizer is likely to turn into a full-course meal."

Derek heaved an exaggerated sigh. "Okay, you win."

When Caroline entered the galley a short time later, the steaks were on the grill and Derek was cutting up ingredients for a salad. "Since it seems you have everything under control here, I'll set the table."

Rooting through the drawers and cupboards, she found candles and holders. "Who needs a restaurant?" she commented. "We can have our own candlelit dinner right here."

Derek came up behind her, sliding his arms around her waist. He nuzzled her neck, murmuring, "Mmmm, you smell better than those steaks."

"Speaking of steaks, don't you think you'd better keep an eye on them before they burn?"

"The steaks are fine," he assured her, but he let his arms drop to his sides and returned to the galley.

He had just placed the steaks on a platter when she joined him. Between the two of them, the meal was on the table within a few minutes. Derek seated her and started toward the other side of the table.

"I almost forgot," he said, snapping his fingers. "I have some wine chilling in the refrigerator. Would you like some?"

Caroline nodded. "That would be nice. We need a match for the candles, too."

A moment later, he returned with the wine, the glasses, and the matches. "I think that's everything," he said, and began to light the candles.

Conversation started with a discussion of the sights they had seen on their various excursions. As the candles burned low, there was a subtle change in the atmosphere. Each time their gazes met it was as if they could read each other's minds, both of them filled with memories. The difference was that they had no need to call on events of years ago.

The passion they had shared that morning was sufficient to occupy their thoughts.

Caroline was unsure if the warmth spreading through her body was the result of the wine or the stares from the man seated across the table. She took a sip of water, which did nothing to douse the smoldering embers inside of her. She was so absorbed by her emotions that Derek had to repeat his question.

"If you're finished, I'll take these dishes."

"Oh, I'll help," she offered.

In no time, the table was cleared. Caroline put the remainder of the wine and salad in the refrigerator as Derek loaded the dishwasher. When she turned from her task, they came face to face with only a few inches separating them.

The opportunity was too tempting to resist and Derek soon had her in his arms. She was wearing a loose-fitting caftan and not much, if anything, else. Her spicy scent engulfed him, briefly bringing to his mind the phrase, "sugar and spice and everything nice."

He leaned against the counter, pulling her closer. Her soft breasts pressed against his chest as his hands slid down her back and halted to cup the flesh of her round derriere. He lowered his head and their lips met in a long, searching kiss.

Caroline slipped her hands under his shirt to caress the smooth skin of his back, the muscles flexing beneath her palms. The heady scent of his cologne surrounded her. She pressed closer to him, immersed in a flood of sensations.

When Derek ended the kiss, Caroline looked up at him and he saw his own desire mirrored in her eyes. "In the interest of safety," he whispered, "I think we'd better continue this in my room."

Caroline nodded and, with their arms around each other's waists, they made their way through the salon and down the hallway. They had barely entered his room when Derek quickly removed his shirt, haphazardly tossing it on a chair. Caroline wasted no time in likewise disposing of her caftan.

Derek's eyes widened slightly and he took a deep breath as he gazed on the tempting curves he had explored thoroughly in the early morning hours. His shorts had barely touched the floor before they were in each other's arms. The embers that had smoldered since early evening immediately burst into flame.

Derek scooped her up in his arms and laid her on the bed and lifted a small packet from the drawer. After a moment of preparation, he lay down beside her, stroking and caressing her emotions into a fever pitch. When she moaned his name, he settled himelf between her warm thighs.

Soon they were caught up in the escalating rhythm that carried them closer and closer to fulfillment. Caroline cried out his name as her body contracted in ultimate pleasure, seconds before he reached his own climax. The fires of passion quenched, they drifted off to sleep in each other's arms.

Derek awakened the next morning with Caroline wrapped in his arms. He lay there contentedly, watching her as she slept. This was where she belonged. She had walked out of his life years ago, and he had let her go because of his foolish suspicion.

Caroline stirred in his arms and drowsily opened her eyes. She yawned and murmured, "Morning."

"Good morning, sweetheart," he murmured, punctuating his greeting with a brief kiss.

"What time is it?" she asked stretching.

Derek glanced at the clock. "Almost nine-fifteen."

She rolled over onto her side and leaned on her elbow.

Placing the palm of her other hand on his chest, she began drawing imaginary circles with the tip of her finger.

"What's on the agenda for today?"

Derek grinned. "If you keep that up, I may not let you let you out of this bed."

She cocked her head to one side. "You seem to have developed a habit of issuing statements like that. I still haven't decided if it's a threat or a promise."

"There's that wanton streak again."

Caroline's answering giggle turned to a shriek when he rolled over, pinning her beneath him. "Now, what was that question?"

"Umm, I asked what's on the agenda."

"That's not the question I'm referring to, and you know it." He nuzzled her neck. "But, in answer to your other question, judging from the moans I heard last night, I don't think it would be much of a threat. I'm sure you know I have no intention of leaving you in this bed alone."

Caroline gasped when he moved slightly and his mouth covered one breast. She writhed in pleasure as the hot moisture from his tongue seemed to flow through her body like molten lava, finally pooling in that most private of places. She whimpered when he abandoned her for a moment. When he returned to her, she clasped him tightly to her and sighed when he entered her a moment later.

"You feel so good," he murmured.

He moved slowly, advancing and retreating, until Caroline thought she would burst. When his hand slipped between their bodies and his fingers stroked the nub that was now the center of her being, she felt as if she had indeed exploded. Wave after wave of exquisite pleasure washed over her.

With one final thrust, Derek cried out her name, joining her in sweet ecstasy. He collapsed on top of her and quickly rolled to his side, still holding her in his arms.

Hearts pounding, they lay in a state of euphoria for a few minutes. Derek was the first to speak. "I don't really plan to keep you locked away all day. So, I guess we should think about getting dressed."

He planted a kiss on her temple, loosened his hold on her, and sat up. "As for the agenda for today, I don't have any particular plans. I thought we'd just drive around, maybe look for that deserted beach on one of the sea islands." He smiled. "Maybe I can still talk you into a little skinny-dipping. If not, at least it'll give you another opportunity to wiggle your toes in the sand."

The day was spent as Derek suggested. They drove to Beaufort and continued across the inlets and creeks to the sea islands. They found the small stretch of beach that Derek had promised and parked the car.

Caroline slipped her feet out of her sandals. "Do you think we'll find any shells?"

"We can try, but I don't think we'll have much luck. The water here seems pretty rough. Most of the shells will probably be broken by the time they reach the beach."

Hand in hand, they strolled the narrow strip of land. As Derek indicated, she found no shells. She was not disappointed though. It was enough to be with him.

As the sun rose high, the heat from its rays rendered their stroll on the beach less inviting. They started walking back toward the car, but Caroline stopped a few feet from the grassy slope. She looked down at her sand-covered feet.

"This is the drawback of strolling in the surf. The wet sand clings and it's not so easy to just brush it off. I can't put my shoes back on with all this sand on my feet."

"There's a bottle of water in the car. You can rinse them off with that."

Soon they were on their way again. They finished their tour of the sea islands and headed back to Beaufort and then to Charleston.

The next day, they visited a few more sights in Charleston.

Over dinner that evening, Derek commented, "I suppose we'd better head back to Savannah tomorrow. When do you plan to leave for Connecticut?"

"Probably Monday or Tuesday. That will give me a few days for the drive and I'll still have a few days at home before school starts."

He nodded. He had known they would have to separate soon, but he was determined to maintain the connection they had reestablished. Years earlier, he had convinced himself that he would get over her eventually. He had already acknowledged that he had been kidding himself all these years. She was a part of him. He would do whatever he had to do to keep from losing her a second time.

They returned to the boat and walked straight to the salon. Before continuing to his room, Caroline turned to him. "Derek, I'm glad you suggested coming along on this trip. This past week has been wonderful."

"That sounds like there's a 'but' coming. What's wrong, Caroline?"

She looked down at the carpeted floor and sighed. Her next words gave voice to his own thoughts. "I'm going back to Connecticut soon and your work is in Atlanta. It's not easy to maintain a long-distance relationship."

Derek cupped her chin, lifting it so that her gaze met his. "I agree that it'll be hard when we're separated by hundreds of miles, but it's not impossible. We've managed to overcome terrible misunderstandings. We can't give up now. I love you, Caroline. I know now that I never stopped loving you.''

Her eyes widened. ''You've never said that before.''

Derek sighed. ''I know. I could never seem to find the courage to say the words. The feelings were there and I convinced myself that you should know how I felt. I've learned since then that it's important to say it.''

Caroline looked down at her feet. ''I guess I have no right to complain about that. I never had the courage to say the words, either.''

''That's true, but I had no doubt of your feelings.''

She looked up and met his steady gaze. ''How could you be so sure?''

Derek cleared his throat. He reached out and caressed her cheek. ''Because I knew you well enough to know that physical intimacy was a serious step for you, then as well as now.''

The heat crept up Caroline's neck and she lowered her gaze.

Derek hugged her. He was careful not let her see him smiling. ''After all we've shared, I can't believe you're blushing. I didn't tell you that to embarrass you.''

She shook her head. ''I'm not embarrassed, just surprised.''

He kissed her tenderly. ''You shouldn't be. I'm very observant when it comes to you. I'm also very determined. Whatever I have to do to make this relationship work, I'll do. I don't want to lose you again. We can make it work if we both think it's worth it.''

He took her hand in his, slowly stroking the knuckles with his thumb. When he spoke again, his voice was barely a whisper.

''I guess what I need to know is whether you think it's worth the effort.''

Caroline lifted her other hand, caressing his cheek. "I don't want to lose you either, Derek." She smiled. "You once said that I was good at ending relationships."

Derek's mood shifted when she smiled. He let out an exaggerated sigh. "I'll never hear the end of that, will I?"

"That's the last time I'll ever mention it. I promise." Her smiled faded. "It wasn't true, though. The hardest thing I ever did was breaking up with you. You should know by now that I think what we have is worth the effort to overcome being separated by a few miles. I just needed to know that you feel as strongly as I do."

She smiled again. "You wouldn't happen to know a cheap airline, would you?"

Derek enfolded her in his arms. "I'm afraid not, but we won't have to worry about that for a while. I'll be coming to Connecticut in October."

"Another computer job?"

He nodded. "What do you say we play it by ear from there?"

"I guess that's all we can do. Do you have any idea how long you'll be there?"

"No, but considering the incentive, Ian may have to drag me back to Atlanta," he said, nuzzling her neck. "Meanwhile, we still have a few days left before you leave for Connecticut."

# Chapter Fourteen

They cruised to Savannah the next day, but decided to spend one more night on the boat before driving back to Atlanta. When Derek questioned her, Caroline could think of no other sight she wanted to see in Savannah. A night in seclusion on the boat sounded much more tempting than any building or structure, no matter how historically significant it might be.

After a day lazing in the sun and a night making love, it was noon before they were on the road to Atlanta. They arrived at Vanessa's early in the evening.

Derek opened the trunk of the car to retrieve her suitcase. Caroline took a few of her other packages in her arms and led the way to the door. She entered the foyer and immediately was met by Vanessa.

"Hey, girlfriend, hi, Derek. How was the trip?"

"Great. I went a little crazy shopping, though," Caroline admitted, setting the bags on the floor.

"Speaking of shopping, I'll get your other packages from the car."

"I almost forgot. The baskets are still in the trunk. I'll come with you."

"Don't bother. I can manage."

"Thanks."

The two women chatted and Caroline pulled a few of her other purchases out of the bag. Derek returned a few minutes later with two large bags.

"Where do you want me to put them?"

"Have you eaten dinner?" Vanessa asked. "You're welcome to stay and join us, Derek."

"We stopped on the way. Thanks anyway."

"In that case, I'll take these upstairs for you," Vanessa offered. "It'll give you two a chance to say good night. That is, if you're planning to say good night here," she added, grinning. "Maybe I'm assuming too much."

Derek cleared his throat and Caroline rolled her eyes. "Just take the packages, Vanessa," she said.

Vanessa laughed and proceeded up the stairs.

Before she was out of sight, Derek's arms were around Caroline. "I have to confess, I was tempted to drive straight to my house."

"What stopped you?"

"I decided I was being selfish and I should give you some time to spend with Vanessa before you go home." He gestured toward the stairs. "After her statement just now, I get the impression that she wouldn't have been upset if I hadn't brought you back until it's time for you to pack to go home."

Caroline smiled. "She's just glad to see us together again."

"So am I," he murmured, just before he kissed her.

Derek broke the kiss when he heard a faint sound on the

stairs. "I guess I'd better say good night, while I still have enough control to let you go. I'll call you tomorrow."

A moment later, he was gone. Caroline picked up her suitcase and started up the stairs as Vanessa appeared on the landing.

"I'll get your other packages," she insisted, passing Caroline on the stairs.

A few minutes later, Vanessa entered the guest room. She placed the packages on the bed and sat down beside them.

"Okay, let's have all the juicy details."

Caroline rolled her eyes. "What makes you think there are any juicy details?"

"I saw the grin on Derek's face when I suggested you might not be ready to say good night yet."

"Let's just say we had wonderful week."

Caroline did give her a few more details about the boat and the cruise and the sightseeing. When she finished, she changed the subject.

"What's happening with you and Kevin?"

"Not much more than a week ago. We've talked a few times and we went out to dinner. I guess I'm being cautious. You know what they say 'once burned, twice shy.' "

Caroline nodded. She leaned over and touched Vanessa's arm. "Just don't get so shy that you're not willing to take a chance."

Vanessa smiled. "I guess that's the voice of experience speaking."

"I don't know about all that. All I can tell you is that it feels right and we're both a little wiser now."


Caroline was up early on Wednesday morning. She and Vanessa had said their good-byes before Vanessa left for work. Half an hour later Caroline opened the door, suitcase in hand, to make her first trip to the car. Derek was on the doorstep, poised to ring the bell. Her eyes widened and the suitcase dropped to the floor.

"What are you doing here?"

Derek raised an eyebrow. "That's a fine greeting."

Caroline smiled. "I'm sorry. You know it's not that I'm not glad to see you. I'm just surprised. I thought we said our good-byes last night."

Derek grinned. "You mean this morning?"

"All right, this morning."

"I decided I had to see you one last time. I knew you were planning to leave early and I felt guilty about keeping you up so late last night."

"I think I had something to do with that decision." She picked up her suitcase again.

Derek took it from her hand. "I'll take this. If you give me your keys, I'll put it in the trunk while you get some of your other things."

She handed over the keys and started back up the stairs. She reached the bottom of the stairs as he returned to the house.

"Is that it?"

"No, there are a few more still upstairs."

"We might as well get the rest of them and we can do this in one trip."

Fifteen minutes later, the car was packed. Caroline locked the door to the house and slipped the keys through the mail slot. She returned to where Derek stood waiting, but did not get into the car. Instead, she stopped a foot away from him.

"Well, I guess that's it."

Derek closed the space between them. "I guess so." He took her in his arms and kissed her much too briefly.

"I'll miss you," she murmured, swallowing hard.

"Sweetheart, not as much as I'll miss you. I just keep

reminding myself that I'll see you in about six weeks, or sooner." He caressed her cheek. "You know I'm not crazy about your driving all the way to Connecticut alone."

"Derek, I drove down here alone and I've already been through this with my family. I'll stop every day before dark. I'll be careful, I promise."

"Will you call me every evening?"

"Yes, I'll call every evening."

He loosened his embrace and reached into his pocket. Handing her a card, he instructed, "My office number is on the front and my home number and cell phone number are on the back."

Caroline nodded.

Derek held the car door open while she settled herself in the driver's seat. He leaned over and kissed her cheek before closing the door. Standing on the sidewalk, he watched until her car was out of sight.

Caroline brushed away a tear. Like Derek, she reminded herself that she would see him in October.


On Friday evening Caroline entered her town house and set her suitcase on the floor. After unloading the car and carrying her suitcases and packages upstairs, she dialed her parents' number.

"I'm at home, Mom," she said as she began to unpack.

"How was your vacation? Although, from what you explained, I guess it was only part vacation."

"It was great, even the tutoring. Actually, I was working less than half the time I was there and the center closed down two weeks ago. I drove to Savannah and then took a trip to Charleston last week."

After telling her that Vanessa had not accompanied her to Savannah, Caroline was glad her mother asked only a few more questions about that trip. She felt a little guilty about letting her parents believe that she had made the trip alone, but she was not ready to discuss her relationship with Derek.

When Caroline entered her town house the following week, she set her tote bag and purse on the hall table and slipped her feet out of her shoes. Padding to the kitchen in her stockinged feet, she opened the refrigator and pulled out a soda. She carried it to the living room, where she plopped down on the sofa.

The first week of school was always exhausting. After a few minutes of relaxation, she rose from the sofa. Retrieving her tote bag and purse, she started up the stairs.

An hour later, somewhat refreshed by a brief shower, she descended the stairs and made her way to the kitchen. She had finished dinner and loaded the dishwasher when the telephone rang. She smiled when she recognized Derek's voice on the other end.

They talked for a few minutes before Derek commented, "You sound tired. Rough week?"

Caroline laughed. "The first week is always a little rough. I'll survive."

They talked for more than an hour. Neither had any information of consequence to share, but they were reluctant to break the connection. When they finally hung up, Caroline sat staring at the telephone for a few minutes, smiling. Derek just might be right about being able to continue a long-distance relationship. Of course, considering they had spoken to each other almost every day that week, their telephone bills might bankrupt them.

* * *

The rest of the month followed the same pattern. Caroline
had not mentioned her relationship with Derek before she
visited her parents in late September.

After dinner, they remained seated at the table, chatting,
when her mother again raised the subject of her summer
vacation. Caroline remembered the photos she had taken
and went to retrieve them from her bag.

Her mother flipped through the pictures. "Is this
Vanessa?" she asked, holding up a snapshot Caroline had
taken on one of their outings.

Caroline nodded.

"She hasn't changed. Of course, it's only been, what, six
years. How's she doing—with the separation and all?"

Her parents had met her former roommate when she visited them in Connecticut and again when Caroline graduated.
She had informed them of Kevin and Vanessa's separation
months ago.

Caroline shrugged. "She's okay. I talked to her a few
days ago. She and Kevin have started formal counseling.
He seems determined to reconcile, but she's wavering. I
think the counseling is her way of trying to gain some
assurance that he's serious about compromising."

Grace took a sip of her tea and focused her attention on
the photos. "And what about you, dear. Did you meet any
interesting men in Atlanta?"

Caroline almost choked on her water. She had deliberately
left out the photos that included Derek. "Umm, well, actually no, I didn't really meet any new men. I did run into
Derek Roberts, though."

"The young man you dated when you were in college?"

Caroline nodded. "His sister-in-law is the teacher I replaced at the center."

Grace looked up. "That's quite a coincidence. You didn't know about this before?"

She shook her head. "Not a clue. I didn't even know Zoe's name until I met her my first day at the center."

Grace asked no more questions about Derek. Being the mother of four, she had learned when not to probe. She suspected there was more involved where this young man was concerned than her daughter had ever revealed.

She recalled how excited Caroline had been when they were dating and how hard she had tried to hide her disappointment when they broke up. If her daughter was closely involved with Derek, Grace could only hope she would not end up being disillusioned.


The second week in October, Caroline received another of the many calls she had received from Derek. It was Friday evening and she was in the process of correcting a stack of test papers when the telephone rang.

After they had dispensed with greetings, Derek asked, "Are you very busy tonight?"

"Not especially, I'm in the process of correcting papers. Why?"

"Well, I was considering coming over, but maybe this isn't a good time."

Caroline took a deep breath and sat straight up. "Are you saying you're here in town?"

"That's right."

"Why didn't you let me know you were coming?"

"I wanted to surprise you."

"How soon will you be here?"

Derek chuckled. "I guess that means this is a good time."

"Of course, it's a good time."

"I'll see you soon, sweetheart."

Caroline had just cleared away the papers from the sofa and put her empty glass in the sink when the doorbell rang. Her eyes widened when she looked through the peephole. She opened the door and within seconds, she was in his arms.

Their lips met in a long, searching, lingering kiss. They were both breathless when he raised his head, breaking the kiss.

"I've missed you," they both blurted out at the same time. Seemingly rooted to the spot, they stared and smiled at each other for a long moment.

Caroline was the first to recover her senses. "How did you get here so fast?" she asked, leading him toward the living room.

Derek grinned. Removing his jacket and hanging it on the coat rack in the small foyer, he explained, "I called from the car. I headed here straight from the airport. I decided if you happened to be out, I'd simply camp on your doorstep until you came home."

She turned to face him again when they reached the sofa. "You could have given me some warning," she said, smoothing her hair. "A long day at school and an evening of grading papers aren't exactly conducive to looking one's best for company."

Derek stared into her eyes and then stepped back, holding her at arms' length. His gaze traveled slowly up and down her robe-clad figure.

"If you're fishing for a compliment, you've got it. You're the most beautiful sight I've seen in more than a month."

Caroline's pulse rate accelerated as his heated gaze seemed to see through the fabric shielding her body. She stepped closer and reached up, caressing his cheek. "If I'm the most beautiful sight, you certainly run a close second."

His arms at her waist, Derek backed up a few inches, pulling her toward him. He then sat down on the sofa, pulling her down onto his lap. He immediately drew her into his arms and the emotions that had been denied for weeks erupted in a blaze of passion. Within minutes, her robe lay in a puddle on the floor. His lips trailed soft wet kisses down her neck and across her collarbone while his hands slowly stroked her skin, rediscovering the curves and valleys he knew he would never tire of exploring.

Caroline fumbled with buttons of his shirt. She could feel the rigid heat of his arousal beneath her. "I want to touch you," she whispered breathlessly.

Derek eased her onto the sofa and stood up. His gaze was riveted to her naked body as he satisfied her request. He quickly shed his own clothes, after retrieving a small packet from the pocket of his trousers. A moment later he lay down beside her. His arms encircled her waist and eased her body over until she lay full length atop his body.

In the few minutes that she had lain alone on the sofa, Caroline had shivered slightly from the cool air in the room. Now her body felt as though it was on fire. She planted kisses along his jawline and nuzzled his neck. With her hands braced on either side of him, her breasts grazed the sprinkling of hairs on his chest. She trembled when his hands clasped the round cheeks of her bottom.

Derek raised one hand, placing it behind her neck and pulling her head down until their lips were less than an inch apart. He outlined her lips with his tongue while his hands continued stroking and kneading her buttocks. He moaned softly when she opened her mouth and began circling his tongue with her own.

He eased her legs apart. She gasped, arching her torso,

when his fingers began slowly stroking her hard, sensitive nub. Caroline groaned, clasping his shoulders as his tongue began laving the nipples of her breasts.

He urged her knees forward and entered her. His hands at her waist guided her into his rhythm of long, deep strokes. Soon, his thrusts came harder and faster.

Caroline murmured his name over and over, pleading for release. He answered her plea with one final stroke propelling them both over the edge. She collapsed on top of him, unable to move or speak. His hands continued to caress her in long sweeps from her back to her thighs.

The temperature in the room seemed to drop with the cooling of their desire. Caroline shivered slightly.

"I could be content to stay right here for a very long time, but I think you're in danger of catching a cold from the draft."

He rolled onto his side and pulled her toward him so that they lay face to face on their sides. With the sofa at her back and his warm body in front of her, he eliminated any possibility of a draft reaching her.

Caroline kissed his chin. "If I had known to expect this, I'd have turned up the thermostat."

"That wouldn't have been as much fun," he observed, hooking his leg over hers. They lay there a while longer, silently savoring the closeness. Then he sighed. "I probably should get up and get dressed."

"Why?" she murmured, snuggling closer.

Derek chuckled. "For one thing, I haven't even checked in at the hotel yet. I couldn't wait to see you."

Caroline started tracing circles on his chest. "You could always wait until Sunday," she suggested. "You don't have to work until Monday, right?"

Derek leaned back a few inches to look her in the eye. "Right. I have to admit, I'd like nothing better than to spend the weekend here with you. Are you sure I wouldn't be imposing?''

"I don't believe you asked that question."

"In that case, I'd better call the hotel and let them know I won't be checking in until Sunday." He rolled over and sat up on the edge of the sofa. He leaned over and planted a kiss between her breasts.

"If you'll show me the way, I think a shower is in order." His warm breath teased her nipples, sending shivers through her body. "In fact, rather than just show me the way, how about joining me?"

Rising from his seat, he held out his hand. Without any hesitation, Caroline placed her hand in his and allowed him to pull her up from the sofa. Gathering their discarded garments, he followed her through the living room and up the stairs.

When they reached her bedroom, Caroline turned to him. "When's the last time you had a bubblebath?"

"I was probably about six years old."

"Hmm, not manly enough?"

Derek chuckled and nodded. "I think you're about to change that opinion."

It was no surprise to either of them that the sensual bath became a prelude to an even more pleasurable activity. Passion's appetite appeased once again, they lay wrapped in each other's arms in her bed.

"So, what do you think about bubblebaths now?" Caroline asked, stifling a yawn.

"You've converted me, but only as long as you're sharing it with me."

"As long as I'm the only one sharing them with you, you have a deal."

Derek's hand caressed the silky skin of her back and he kissed her temple. "I wouldn't have it any other way, baby."

* * *

The next morning, Caroline awoke first. For a few minutes, she lay quietly watching him sleep before easing from the bed.

Derek was awakened by the sound of running water. He opened his eyes slowly and looked around the unfamiliar room. Memories of the previous day flooded into his mind. He squelched the temptation to join her in the shower and lay patiently waiting for her to return.

Caroline exited the bathroom clad in a robe and stopped abruptly when she encountered his heated gaze. Quickly recovering her composure, she commented, "Oh, you're awake. The shower's all yours."

"You mean we can't take another bubble bath?"

Caroline shook her head and smiled. "I'll go start breakfast while you shower. There are towels in the closet behind the door."

Derek rubbed his stomach. "I guess a little nourishment is in order."

After a brief shower, he made a quick trip to the car to retrieve his bag and headed back up the stairs. Half an hour and a change of clothes later, he joined Caroline in the kitchen.

Helping himself to coffee, he commented, "I thought you didn't eat breakfast."

"I usually don't. You'll realize that when you see what I have to offer. The best I can come up with is a cheese omelet and bagels."

"That sounds good to me."

When they entered the living room after breakfast, Caroline discovered the unfinished schoolwork she had shoved aside the previous evening. She groaned and looked at Derek.

"I wish I could put this off again, but I don't dare. We seem to get distracted too easily."

He smiled. "Don't feel guilty. I'm the one who interrupted your work." He hugged her to his side and kissed her temple. "I'm just glad to be here with you."

# Chapter Fifteen

*Atlanta*

Cal parked the unobtrusive rental car at the curb and opened the door. He got out and locked the door. As he approached the dilapidated building, he scanned the area, not that he expected to see any of his acquaintances in this part of town.

He opened the outer door of the building and flinched slightly from the stench in the hallway. Walking slowly while his eyes adjusted to the darkness, he made his way up the stairs. He knocked twice and the door was opened immediately.

"Hey man, you was supposed to be here a hour ago."

"I got tied up."

"So what's the deal?"

"All in good time, D.C." He scanned the room, lit only by two battery powered lamps. "Where's JoJo?"

"He's in the back room. He don't like waitin' around in this dump. Neither do I."

"I'm not interested in what either of you like or don't like. I'm about to make you two rich. I think that entitles me to have my intructions followed."

Just then, JoJo entered from the back room. "It's about time you got here. We been stuck in this room waitin' for you."

"As I just told your friend," Cal replied through clenched teeth, "I'm the man who's going to make you rich. So, maybe you need to learn a little patience."

JoJo opened his mouth to retort, but D.C. nudged him. "Chill. He's here now. Let's find out what it's all about."

"Yeah, yeah, whatever." He turned to Cal. "So what are you payin' us to do?"

"All you have to do is grab a certain lady, bring her here, and keep her here. I'll do the rest."

"Kidnapping! You want us to kidnap someone?" JoJo backed away a few steps. "Uh-uh, man. I ain't gettin' mixed up with no Feds."

Cal looked at D.C. and inclined his head in JoJo's direction. "This is the man you said wasn't afraid of anything?"

"He'll change his mind when you tell him how much you're gonna pay us," D.C. assured him. "Just let me talk to him."

"You should have made sure of him before. I don't like being put in this position after telling you my plans."

D.C. turned to his friend. "Look man, we're talkin' about fifty big ones, each. It ain't no thing. We grab the chick, get our money, and roll."

"And what's he gettin'?"

Cal broke into their conversation. "What I'm getting is none of your concern. I'm setting this up. I'm arranging for the payoff. Your part is minor. You two big tough men can't handle one woman? All you have to do is bring her here and keep her in the back room until I get the money.''

When they hesitated, Cal sneered and shook his head. ''Forget it. I'm sure I can find someone else who's willing to do this simple job in return for fifty thousand dollars.''

''Okay, okay. You got it. Just make sure this plan is foolproof.''

Cal stared at the two men for a minute. He almost regretted involving these slow-witted hoods in his master plan. He reminded himself that their slow wits were the very traits that would work in his favor.

''Let's get down to business, then.''

The next hour was spent going over the details of their part in the kidnapping. When he had originally plotted his revenge, he'd considered kidnapping Ian himself. He'd quickly discarded that plan. It might be too difficult for Ian's family and friends to raise the money. Ian would be able to get the funds much more quickly and, once Cal had Zoe in his grasp, time would be an important factor. After he had the money in his possession, he would waste no time getting out of town and out of the country.

''So, all we got to do is follow this chick and wait for our chance to grab her?''

''That's right. There's a chance she'll be driving one of two cars. I'll give you a description of both cars and the license plate numbers. Remember, no kids, they're too much trouble. Wait until she's alone.''

Cal pulled out a slip of paper. ''Here's the address, the cars' descriptions, and plate numbers. The other address is a community center she visits regularly. If you start following her when she leaves home, you should be able to grab her somewhere along the way.''

Cal left them a few minutes later. He returned to his car, surveying his surroundings once again. The area and the nearly deserted building would be perfect. The only other occupants were a few homeless squatters. Even if one of them noticed something suspicious, they were unlikely to get involved.

He looked up at the dimly lit window of the apartment where he had just left the two men. He recalled his first meeting with them. He was glad now that he had not followed his initial inclination to tell John to shove it when he suggested the meetings. Meeting those two thugs had been the only satisfaction he had derived from those tedious meetings.

D.C.'s response to the amount of the payment Cal offered told Cal that he could count on his cooperation. Cal thought it was ironic that D.C.'s only condition was not being involved in murder. That was no problem. If Cal decided it was necessary, he would handle that job himself.

Ian's secretary, Karla, buzzed the intercom. "Derek's on line two."

"Thanks," Ian replied, picking up the receiver. "How's the job coming, Derek?"

"I ran into some trouble. I'll probably be here until the end of the month. Is that a problem?"

Ian smiled. "That trouble wouldn't have anything to do with having Caroline in close proximity, would it?"

"No, big brother, it has nothing to do with Caroline."

"Speaking of Caroline, how's it going? Or is that none of my business?"

"It's going great and I wouldn't tell you it's none of your business. At least not in those words."

Ian chuckled. "I'm sure you'd put it more tactfully, but it would be the same message."

"Seriously, Ian, I'm sure you know that you and Zoe

were partly responsible for the discussion that cleared up the misunderstandings between us. I don't think I ever thanked you for that.''

"Don't mention it. I owed you one. Besides, we brothers have to look out for each other."

"In that case, do you have any advice for me? I'm meeting her parents this weekend."

"I'm afraid you're on your own with that one. All I can do is wish you luck. I remember the first time I met Zoe's parents. Her parents weren't the difficult ones, though. Even her brothers weren't as intimidating as her sister. Cleo was the one who made me nervous. It was obvious she was skeptical about my motives."

"Thanks for reminding me that I still have to deal with the brothers and sister. Fortunately, that won't come until late—hopefully, much later."

"Well, I can't help you with the personal problems, but if you need my input about the job, give me a call."

"Will do."


Derek recalled that conversation as they drove to New Haven. He had no idea how much Caroline's parents knew about him. They knew that the two of them had dated when she was in college. That revelation did nothing to ease his mind.

After a few minutes of anxiety, he determinedly put those thoughts aside and concentrated on what became a pleasant, scenic drive. From what he knew of her parents, they were reasonable people. What had happened between Caroline and him years ago had no bearing on the present. He only hoped that they agreed.

They pulled into her parents' driveway shortly after noon. He got out of the car and went around to help her out.

Caroline led the way up the walk and rang the doorbell. It was opened by her father, who greeted her with a hug. Her mother joined them in the foyer a moment later and Caroline performed the introductions before they were ushered into the living room.

"Caroline tells us you're a computer expert. You're in Connecticut on business?"

"That's right. I'm installing a security system for one of the insurance companies. There's a big problem these days with hackers."

"I've read a few newspaper articles about people breaking into computer systems. Will your security system solve the problem?"

Derek shrugged. "We certainly hope so, but we can't ever be absolutely sure. These hackers are extremely intelligent. It's too bad they don't put that intelligence to a more productive use."

Grace smiled as Derek went into one of his monologues on computers. He reminded her of her son, Jason. The smallest comment could send him off on a tangent about architecture.

Before long, the relaxed and comfortable atmosphere created by Caroline's parents relieved Derek's tension. It was only natural that they would be concerned for their daughter's emotional welfare. Since that was also his concern, he had no reason to be nervous.

Caroline had a moment of apprehension when her mother raised the topic of her trip to Savannah. It would have required some fast explaining if her parents learned, at this late date, that Derek had accompanied her.

The fact that they asked him nothing of the trip and the wary expression in Caroline's eyes helped Derek put two and two together. It was understandable that she would omit the fact that he had traveled to Savannah with her. He winked at her and could almost hear her sigh of relief.

Caroline mentioned that conversation on their way back to Hartford. "Thanks for not giving me away. When I told them I had gone to Savannah, I neglected to mention a few of the details." She glanced at him. "I hope you're not upset about that."

Derek grinned. "I'm not upset. I suppose telling them we spent the week together on my boat might lead to questions you'd rather not answer."

Caroline shook her head slowly. "They wouldn't actually ask any questions." She cocked her head to one side. "Actually, it's not even that they would disapprove. Maybe it's just that there are certain things that should be private, even from one's parents."

Derek nodded. "That's a good way to put it." He took one hand from the wheel, placing it on her knee. "I agree that some things should definitely remain private."


After Caroline and Derek had driven away, Harry turned to Grace. "Do you feel better now?"

"What do you mean, dear?"

Harry chuckled and put his arm around his wife. "Do you think after almost forty years of marriage, I don't know when you're worried? I know you've been concerned ever since you learned that Derek was back in Caroline's life."

Grace shrugged. "Until a few days ago, I wasn't sure to what extent he was back in her life."

He nodded. "I don't think there's any doubt now." He squeezed her shoulder. "So, back to my first question. Do you feel better now?"

She looked up at him, smiling. "Yes, I do. I don't know what happened between them before, but it's obvious that he cares for her." She cocked her head to one side. "What do you think?"

"Unless my ability to read people has deserted me completely, I'd say the young man is very much in love with our daughter."

For several weeks, Caroline and Derek cherished their time together. Neither one allowed the impending separation to intrude on their happiness. Almost every weekend was spent together, either at Caroline's house or in Derek's hotel room. The only exception was when Derek suggested a trip to New Hampshire for the holiday weekend.

Caroline arranged a stay at an inn that afforded them a view of Mt. Washington. They had little interest in sightseeing, but they made an exception when the manager of the inn suggested the scenic railway ride up the mountainside. Other than that, they were content to enjoy the colorful fall foliage as they strolled the winding pathways arm in arm.

After an early dinner on Sunday, they took another short stroll and retired to their room. He helped her off with her coat and then went to the gas fireplace and turned it on.

"I'm glad you requested a room with a fireplace," he commented, adjusting the flame to a comfortable level.

"Why? It's not that cold in here."

"Not at the moment," he admitted, coming toward her. Unbuttoning her sweater, he added, "But, that might change after I relieve you of this cumbersome clothing."

"There's always the bedcovers, you know," she reminded him.

"Not for what I have in mind." He glanced at the assortment of oversized pillows near the fireplace.

Within minutes, their clothes lay draped on the chair and Derek eased her to the floor in front of the fire. The flickering flames were the only light in the room. When he joined her on the floor, Caroline sat up. Derek raised an eyebrow.

"I never seem to get a chance to explore as much as I'd like. This time it's my turn."

Derek grinned and folded his hands behind his head. "Be my guest, sweetheart."

Kneeling beside him, her hands slowly roamed over his chest and torso, before moving lower. Her fingers played in the mat of hair surrounding his shaft as she leaned over his body, her tongue drawing circles around his nipples.

Caroline sat up and reached across him, picking up the small packet he had placed on the table nearby. "Shall I take care of this for you?"

Derek grinned. "Are you sure you can manage?"

She shrugged. "You can always assist me if I'm doing it wrong."

Derek groaned deep in his throat when her fingers encircled his member before sliding the thin covering over it. He slid his hands from under his head and reached for her breasts, kneading the soft flesh.

"Am I doing this right?" Caroline asked, trying very hard to concentrate on her task.

"Sweetheart, if your aim is to drive me crazy, you're doing just fine."

Caroline resumed her caresses, but not for long. She gasped when Derek's other hand came to rest on the triangle of hair between her thighs. When his fingers slipped inside her, she ceased her own explorations.

Clutching his shoulders, she whispered, "You don't play fair."

Derek chuckled. "It's self-defense. My control isn't unlimited."

A moment later, she was lying on the floor cushions. He eased his body between her silky thighs. His lips met hers as he entered her swiftly and deeply. Soon, they were engaged in the familiar rhythm that had brought them to ecstasy so many times before. This time was no different. They cried out in unison, exalting in the currents of pleasure that coursed through them.

Two weeks after their weekend in New Hampshire, Caroline and Derek were faced with the inevitable. Derek arrived on Friday with take-out food for dinner. They had finished dinner and were relaxing in the living room, listening to music, when he broke the news to her.

"I finished the job today."

Caroline had been leaning against his shoulder, his arm encircling her. She glanced up at him and sighed. There was no need to ask what his remark meant.

"When do you leave for Atlanta?"

He kissed her temple. "Monday morning."

Caroline bit her lip. "Well, we knew this was coming."

"What are my chances of convincing you to come to Atlanta for Thanksgiving?"

Caroline sat up. "It's not a matter of convincing me to come. The problem is that's a busy time of year for traveling. I'm not sure I can even get an airline ticket or a hotel."

Derek stifled the first thought that came to his mind. For whatever reason, she evidently did not feel comfortable staying with him.

"What about Vanessa—as far as the hotel is concerned, that is?"

She shook her head. "She and Kevin just reconciled a few days ago. I don't think it would be a good idea for them to have a houseguest any time soon."

"If that's the only problem, I suggest we start working on it. It's almost a month away. Maybe we'll get lucky."

*Atlanta*

Two weeks after giving JoJo and D.C. their assignments, Cal met with them again in the same deserted building. "I can't believe you haven't been able to get this simple job done," he said, pacing the floor.

"Hey, man, it ain't that easy. She always has one of them kids with her and you said you didn't want no kids."

"What about when she goes to the center? Have you been following her like I told you to do?"

"Yeah, we been followin' her. She even has one of them kids when she goes there and there's always a bunch of people around."

Cal ran his hand through his hair. October was almost gone. He had been planning this for months. He considered changing his rules.

If the children were older, it might work. These were young children, though—one of them a toddler. Taking them would be more trouble than it was worth.

He had almost discarded the idea of harming his victim, deciding the money and the anxiety caused by the kidnapping would be sufficient revenge. Noisy, crying kids might force him to change those plans. He was no killer, but if he were forced to dispose of Zoe, he could do it. Killing kids was different, though. He had no stomach for that.

He had to be patient. He had waited almost five years for this. He could wait a little longer.

"Okay, just make sure you stay on her tail. There's bound to be some time when she's alone."

# Chapter Sixteen

Derek arrived in Atlanta early Monday morning. After stopping at home to unpack, he drove to the office and went directly to Ian's private office. His brother was seated at the computer and he turned to greet him when he walked in.

"Hey, Derek. I didn't expect to see you today. I thought you'd take the rest of the day off."

Derek shrugged and sat down. "I didn't see any point in doing that. How's everything here? Any more problems with the nine-one-one system?"

"None. Let's hope it stays that way."

"How're Zoe and the kids?"

"Fine. I think having the summer off did her a lot of good, but I don't think she'll ever admit it." He left the computer and took the seat at his desk across from his brother. "How's Caroline? How was your dinner with her parents?"

"Caroline's fine and dinner went well. Her parents are

very nice people. They have a way making a person feel at home." He cleared his throat. "I have a favor to ask of you and Zoe."

He told Ian about Caroline's anticipated visit and her plan to stay at a hotel. "Is there any chance she can stay with you?"

Ian smiled. "Well, since I already said we brothers have to look out for each other, I think I can arrange that. I'm sure Zoe will be happy to see her again and to be able to spend more time with her."

Derek rubbed his chin. "There's just one other thing. She'll never accept if I call and suggest it. The invitation will have to come from Zoe."

"I don't think that'll be a problem, but don't you think she might suspect you put her up to it?"

"Maybe, but I doubt that she'll come right out and question Zoe."

Ian rose from his seat and came around to the other side of the desk. He put his hand on Derek's shoulder. "She's obviously very important to you. I hope it works out for you this time."

"Thanks, Ian. She is very important to me. I don't intend to make the same mistake twice."

A week after Derek returned to Atlanta, Caroline received a telephone call from Zoe. "Hi, Caroline. Derek said you're planning to come to Atlanta for Thanksgiving. He also said you were planning to stay at a hotel. I hope you'll change your mind about that. You're welcome to stay with us."

"Thanks, Zoe, but that's not necessary. When we discussed it, I told Derek I wasn't sure I'd be able to get a room, but I managed to get a reservation."

"You can always cancel the reservation. Please change your mind. I'd really like to have you stay with us."

Caroline hesitated. She suspected that Derek had had a hand in Zoe's invitation, but neither of them was likely to admit it. There was a chance Zoe might be insulted if Caroline suggested her invitation was only being issued because of Derek.

"Caroline?"

"Yes, I'm still here. I appreciate your offer, Zoe. Are you sure it won't be an inconvenience?"

"I promise you, it's not an inconvenience. I'd really enjoy having a chance for us to get better acquainted." *Especially since there's a very good possibility that you'll be my sister-in-law eventually*, Zoe thought.

"In that case, I accept your offer. I'm looking forward to seeing you again, too."

The two women talked for a few more minutes. Zoe filled her in on the activities at the center. Caroline, in turn, told Zoe about her current class.

After Zoe hung up the telephone, she turned to Ian. "It took a little convincing, but Caroline will be staying here for Thanksgiving."

Ian nodded. "I don't understand why she doesn't stay at Derek's house."

Zoe put her hand on her hip. "You're kidding, right? If she stays with him, it will give people, such as your family, certain ideas about their relationship. Even if they are intimately involved, she may not be ready to have it out in the open."

Ian reached over and pulled her onto his lap, grinning. "You mean people might get ideas like they might have had about our relationship, if they had known the whole truth."

"That was a very different situation," Zoe insisted, frowning.

He nuzzled her neck. "Yes, but they would have been right on target with those ideas you mentioned."

Early in November, Caroline overheard a conversation between two of her students that piqued her interest. It reminded her of the job that had brought Derek to Connecticut. The two girls were discussing the crush one of them had on the other's brother.

"I don't know why you think he's all that," Lisa said. "All he does is sit at that computer all the time. Some of the stuff he gets on it is really wacked."

"Like what?" Keana asked.

Lisa leaned toward her, conspiratorially. "I sneaked into his room once when he left to get something to eat. He had some stuff on the screen from some bank in Seattle."

"What kind of stuff?"

Lisa shrugged. "I don't know. When he came back and caught me in his room, he started trippin'. You'd have thought I broke his computer or something."

"Well, I don't care what you say. You just don't appreciate him 'cause he's your brother."

"Yeah, right. You're wasting your time even thinking about him. He's not interested in anything but computers." Their lunch break over, the two girls gathered up their trash and left the room.

Caroline sat watching them, digesting the information Lisa had unwittingly divulged. She remembered Lisa's brother, Aaron. He had been something of a computer whiz even in the fifth grade.

He was a good kid. She had difficulty believing he was

breaking into computer systems and wreaking the kind of havoc Derek had described. He must be one of those people who broke into the systems just for the thrill of knowing he could do it.

Whatever his reasons for hacking, he had to be made to understand that what he was doing was wrong and could get him into serious trouble. Derek might be just the one who could get that message across.

That evening she called Derek, and told him about the conversation between her students.

"I don't like the sound of that. I had a call from the insurance company whose security system I installed in March. Someone tried to get into the system and they almost traced him, but he went offline before they could finish the trace."

"You can't be sure it was Aaron. Lisa mentioned a bank in Seattle, of all places."

"No, I can't be sure he's the one, but if he's breaking into bank systems in Seattle, he could easily be breaking into other sites closer to home."

"I'm just interested in stopping Aaron. Maybe you could talk to him and explain how serious what he's doing could be."

Derek hesitated. "Caroline, there's not much I can do from here."

"If I get his telephone number, you could call him. He'd probably look up to you if I tell him you're a successful software designer."

"His parents might not appreciate my interference."

It was obvious he was hesitant to become involved. "I can't think of any reason why they'd object."

"It's possible they'd see it as an accusation."

"I hadn't thought about it from that angle. Maybe you're

right, but there must be some way to get through to him if you explain the problem to them. Will you think about it?''

He sighed. ''I'll think about it, sweetheart.''


Concern for the boy was still in the back of her mind when Caroline boarded the plane for Atlanta two weeks later. She had given Derek his family's telephone number, but she doubted that Derek had called. She had spoken with him several times since then, and he never mentioned it.

Caroline spied Derek's smiling face immediately when she came through the gate. A few minutes later she was in his arms. She leaned up on her toes and kissed him briefly, drawing a few stares from the crowd around them.

''How was your flight?'' he asked, taking her tote bag.

''Fine,'' she assured him.

He took her arm, steering her toward the baggage area. ''Are you hungry? I thought we'd stop for lunch before we go to Ian's.''

She nodded. ''That sounds good.''

Two hours later, seated in the restaurant, Caroline turned to Derek. ''What time is Zoe expecting us?''

Derek shrugged. ''No specific time. I told her I'd call if we expected to be there for dinner.''

He reached across the table and took her hand in his, gently stroking the knuckles with his thumb. Caroline watched the movement that was sending a familiar tingle up her arm. Then she looked up and met his intent gaze.

''I could call her and tell her not to expect us until dinner tomorrow.''

Caroline licked her lips. ''What about dinner tonight?''

''Well, I'm sure I could manage something, or we could order in. Whichever we decide, I promise to satisfy your appetite, or maybe I should say 'appetites.' ''

Just then the waiter approached the table. Derek let go of her hand and paid the check. They left the restaurant, and he paused when they reached his car.

"You never answered my question," he reminded her, holding the passenger door open.

Caroline moved closer to him. "As I recall, it wasn't a question at all, but a suggestion." She reached up to stroke his bottom lip with her thumb. "But to answer you, the meal I just consumed didn't seem to satisfy me completely."

She replaced her thumb with her mouth. This time it was not a brief hello kiss, but a prelude to what awaited them a short drive away.

When they arrived at Derek's house, he drove into the garage and popped the trunk open. With her bags in his hands, he led her through to the front hall and up the stairs. He immediately set her luggage just inside the bedroom, freeing his hands for a more pleasant exercise.

His arms encircled her and their lips met, hot and hungry. Soon they were engaged in fulfilling the desires that mere food could not satisfy.

Much later, they lay naked in each other's arms. Caroline sighed. "You'd better call Zoe before she starts to think we've met with some disaster."

Derek chuckled. "You mean like that earthquake that just shook the house."

He rolled over and picked up the telephone receiver and dialed his brother's number. When Ian answered, he said, "I promised Zoe I'd let her know whether to expect us for dinner today. I hope she won't be upset that we decided not to come today at all. What time is dinner tomorrow?"

"Around three o'clock."

"We'll be there well before that time, probably between noon and one o'clock."

"That's fine, Derek. I'm sure Zoe won't be upset." He chuckled. "We wouldn't want to interfere with your reunion with Caroline."

"Thanks, we'll see you tomorrow."


Ian greeted them at the door when they arrived shortly before one o'clock for Thanksgiving dinner. He hugged Caroline.

"It's good to see you again."

Derek took her bags up to the guest room while Ian ushered her into the family room. Zoe joined them while he was in the process of reintroducing Caroline to his parents who had arrived two days earlier.

"It's great to see you again," Zoe said, smiling. She turned to the woman just behind her. "You haven't met Ian's sister, Elizabeth. This is Caroline Duval."

Elizabeth nodded. "You're the teacher who covered for Zoe at the center this summer, right? Zoe's told me a bit about you. It's nice to finally meet you."

Just then Derek joined them. "I hung your garment bag in the closet."

"If you'll excuse me," Zoe interrupted. "I'd better check on the turkey."

"Can I help?" Caroline offered.

Elizabeth nudged her. "I already offered. I don't think she trusts anyone else's cooking."

Zoe laughed and shook her head. "That's not true. I'm trying to be a good hostess. I wouldn't mind company, though."

Caroline and Elizabeth followed her to the kitchen. Caroline sniffed the air as they entered the room.

"Mmm, it smells delicious."

"Have a seat. Would you like a drink? There are sodas, coffee, or tea."

"Actually, just water would be fine."

"I'll get it, Zoe," Elizabeth said.

She filled two glasses with ice and water. After setting one in front of Caroline, she took the other and sat down across from her.

As she basted the turkey, Zoe said, "When Ian gave me Derek's message, I thought maybe you had changed your mind and decided to stay at Derek's."

Caroline glanced at Elizabeth, who averted her eyes and nonchalantly sipped her water. Zoe's back was to them, so she missed the expression on her guest's face.

Zoe closed the oven door and looked over at Caroline, who had not quite regained her poise. "I'm sorry. Maybe I shouldn't have said that. I hope I didn't embarrass you."

Caroline shook her head. "No, Zoe. You just caught me off guard. You knew I stayed there last night, so it was a reasonable question." She looked at Elizabeth. "Since I arrived today with Derek, it wouldn't be difficult to put two and two together."

Zoe thought it best to move on to a different topic. "Well, since you're staying here tonight, how do you feel about going shopping with me tomorrow?"

"Are you one of those Black Friday shoppers?"

Zoe nodded. "That's right. Every year, and every year Ian shakes his head and tells me I must be crazy." She set the baster on the counter and walked toward the table. "Of course, this is coming from a man who does all of his shopping on Christmas Eve."

Caroline laughed. She turned to Elizabeth. "Are you coming with us?"

Elizabeth shook her head. "Not on your life. You two

can have that pleasure all to yourselves. Except that the problem is you'll have more than enough company.''

A few minutes later, they rejoined the others in the family room. Elizabeth pondered Zoe's earlier statement as she observed her brother. She must be the only one in the family who had been in the dark about Derek's new relationship until now. A few of the other women he previously dated had accompanied him to family gatherings, but his feelings had never before been as obvious as they were every time he looked at Caroline.


Derek was placed between Caroline and Savannah when they sat down to dinner. Derek had told her some of the stories of his niece's antics and she now saw firsthand what he meant when he said her parents had their hands full.

After dinner, they retired to the family room and their conversation inevitably turned to the topic of computers. Ian mentioned the call from the insurance company regarding the attempt to break into their computers. His comment reminded Caroline of her request to Derek.

She brought up the subject as they were saying good night. ''I guess you never called Aaron.''

Derek sighed. ''I didn't think it would make any difference, Caroline. Anyway, if he's actually done damage to one of the sites he's broken into, maybe he needs to find out the hard way that it's not fun and games.''

''By going to jail? That was the whole idea in my asking you to talk to him. You might be able to make him see how serious it is before he does any real damage.''

''Caroline . . .''

She folded her arms in front of her. ''Forget it, Derek. I don't agree with you, but Aaron's not your responsibility. I had no right to try to involve you.''

One look at her told him there was no point in trying to explain any further. He leaned over and kissed her cheek.

"Will you call me when you and Zoe get back from your shopping trip tomorrow?"

"Yes, Derek. I'll call you."

# Chapter Seventeen

Caroline awoke the next morning to the smell of coffee and Ian's voice admonishing his daughter to stop running in the hallway. His warning was followed by a small voice that sounded suspiciously unrepentant. Her father was not taken in by her performance. Caroline smiled and shook her head at the subtle difference in Savannah's voice when she responded to Ian's second warning.

The hall was empty when Caroline entered the bathroom a few minutes later. She had had a restless night. She was angry with herself for trying to coerce Derek into contacting Aaron. If he truly believed that Aaron had to learn his lesson the hard way, he would probably do more harm than good by talking to him.

The shower revived her spirits. As she dressed, she pushed aside thoughts of Aaron and Derek and resolved to concentrate on shopping.

When she entered the kitchen, the scene reminded Caroline of the holidays at her own parents' home. Elizabeth was pouring coffee for her mother, while Ian and Zoe worked side by side at the stove.

Blake sat in his high chair, intermittently munching toast and pounding his juice cup on the tray. Savannah was engrossed in deep conversation. Caroline only caught a few words, but it appeared she was trying to explain her earlier disagreement with her father.

Caroline smiled. "Good morning," she said, walking over to the stove.

"Is there anything I can do to help?"

Zoe shook her head. "Contrary to appearances, everything is under control." She gestured to the coffeepot. "Help yourself to coffee."

Caroline had eaten and was almost finished with her second cup of coffee when Zoe suggested, "Whenever you're ready, I think we should get started, Caroline."

Caroline nodded. "I'm ready when you are."

Zoe rose from the table. She leaned over and kissed Ian. "I'll leave you to deal with the cleanup," she said, smiling.


Neither women noticed the van that followed them from the time they left the house. It tailed them to the mall and then pulled into a parking space two rows away.

"Now what, D.C.? She still ain't alone."

"At least she don't have them kids with her. We'll just have to wait and see where she goes from here."


After a few hours of shopping, Caroline and Zoe returned to the car to deposit their packages. "What do you say we have lunch before we continue? I think a little nourishment is in order."

"That sounds like a good idea. Where do you want to go?"

"I think someplace in the mall. There are a couple of other stores I want to check out."

It was late afternoon when the two women called a halt to their shopping. Laden with bags, they made their way to the car. After they stowed the packages in the trunk, Zoe turned toward Caroline.

"Do you mind if we stop at the center? I want to drop off these toys for the Christmas party." She smiled and touched Caroline's arm. "By the way, thanks for the contribution."

"You're welcome and no, I don't mind stopping at the center. The party sounds like a great idea."

A few minutes later they drove out of the crowded parking lot. Once again, the van pulled out of its spot to trail behind them. As the van approached a traffic light a few blocks from the center, the light changed to red. D.C. stopped the van.

"What you doin', man? We gonna lose 'em."

"Chill, JoJo. All we need is to get pulled over for runnin' a red light. We ain't gonna lose 'em."

Zoe double-parked the car in front of the center. "There's no point in going into the lot. I won't be long. If you don't mind, though, maybe you'd better sit in the driver's seat. If you have to move it, you can just drive around the block."

After a few minutes in the driver's seat, Caroline pulled a notepad from her purse. She jotted down the purchases she had made that day. Along with some of the items she had purchased in Charleston, she had made quite a dent in her Christmas gift list. She looked up when the driver's door opened, expecting to see Zoe. Instead, she was confronted by a man in a ski mask.

Before she could utter a sound, he clapped his hand over

her face. She had barely whiffed the sickening smell emanating from the cloth before she was rendered unconscious. After stuffing the cloth into his pocket, JoJo dragged her from the car just as Zoe exited the building.

"What are you doing?" Zoe screamed. "Leave her alone."

She ran to the side of the van and began pounding on the man and shouting for help. JoJo dumped Caroline in the van. He turned and grabbed Zoe, clapping his hand over her mouth to stifle her screams.

"Gimme some help, man," he yelled to D.C.

"Use the stuff and let's get outta here."

He removed his hand from her mouth long enough to take the cloth from his pocket. With some effort, he managed to slap it over Zoe's face. The chloroform had lost some of its strength, but it was not completely powerless. Zoe struggled for a few seconds before sagging in his arms.

"What now?" he asked.

"Throw her in the van. We gotta roll before someone sees us."

Seconds later, the van sped away.

D.C. drove the van into the alley beside the dilapidated building. He got out and looked around before walking to the side of the van.

"What we gonna do with two of 'em?" JoJo asked. "He only told us to grab one." He looked at the two women lying on the floor of the van. Neither of them had stirred during the ride from the center.

D.C. shrugged. "That's his problem. We couldn't leave the other one there for someone to find. She saw the van. We got the one he wanted. Let him figure it out."

They carried the unconscious women up the stairs to the apartment where they had met with Cal. After dumping them onto a mattress on the floor in the back room, they tied their hands behind their backs. Then they left the room and locked the door behind them.

D.C. took out his cell phone and paged Cal. A few minutes later, Cal called back. "Now what?"

"We got her."

*It's about time*, Cal thought. "Did anyone see you?"

"No, man. We grabbed her at that center. I guess it's closed. No one was around."

"I'll be there in half an hour."

"Where is she?" Cal asked as soon as he walked in the door.

"In the back room," D.C. informed him. "They're still out. That stuff you gave us worked good."

Cal was in such a hurry to see that he finally had Zoe in his grasp that D.C.'s indication that there was more than one victim escaped him. He started toward the back room.

His eyes narrowed when he opened the door and saw the two women lying on the mattress. He pointed to Caroline and then looked at the other man.

"Who's she?"

D.C. frowned. "She's the chick you told us to grab."

He pointed to Zoe. "She's the woman I told you to grab."

"How was we supposed to know? The other one was drivin' the car. When we grabbed her, this chick started screamin', so we took both of 'em."

"So what you're telling me is that you just happened to get the right woman by accident."

"What's the deal, man? We got the chick like you said."

Cal shook his head. "Yeah, right."

"So, when do we get the bread?"

"Soon." He pulled out a camera. "Bring that lamp in here."

Zoe stirred when he snapped the photos, but she did not awaken. Cal quickly left the room and D.C. followed him.

"I'll be back later," Cal said. "They'll probably be awake soon. Take good care of them, they're going to make us rich. Be sure you keep that door locked."

"Hey, man, we ain't stupid. The window's boarded and we tied their hands. They ain't goin' nowhere."

Zoe was the first to awaken soon after Cal left. She shook her head in an effort to clear the remaining effects of the chloroform. Caroline lay nearby, still unconscious.

"Wake up, Caroline," she whispered, nudging her friend with her knee.

Caroline stirred and, after more prodding, opened her eyes. "Zoe? What—what's going on?" she murmured groggily, tugging at the ropes around her wrists.

Zoe took a deep breath. "I think we've been kidnapped."

Caroline shook her head. "I thought he wanted the car." She tried to sit up, but flopped back onto the bed. "I feel sick."

"I think you had quite a dose of whatever it was they used to knock us out. Maybe you should just lie still for a while. When you feel better we'll see if we can get these ropes off."

Ian looked out of the window for the tenth time in the past hour. It was past dinnertime and there had been no word from Zoe. He tried to convince himself that she and Caroline had simply lost track of the time.

With his sister's help, he prepared dinner. He ate little

himself. Both his parents and Elizabeth could see he was worried.

After dinner, the adults moved to the family room and tried to occupy their minds by playing with the children. They had barely settled themselves when the doorbell rang. Ian excused himself and went to answer it.

He opened the door to find a police officer on his doorstep. He felt as if his heart had leaped into his throat.

"Mr. Ian Roberts?"

"Yes, that's right."

When the officer asked about his car, Ian could barely answer his questions. "What about my car? Has there been an accident?"

"Not exactly, sir. We found it double-parked and abandoned. Do you know anything about that?"

"No, my wife was driving it."

"Is she at home?"

"No. You said you found it abandoned. What condition is it in?"

"I don't understand your question."

"Did you examine it?"

"I think I know what you're getting at, sir. There was nothing to indicate violence. It was clean inside. Is there a particular reason you ask?"

Ian sighed and shook his head. "I don't know what's going on, Officer . . ."

"McClellan, sir."

"As I said, I have no idea why my wife left the car." He ran his fingers through his hair. "I don't know what else to say."

"Well, sir, I suppose you could file a missing person report. We don't usually take such reports until the person has been missing for twenty-four hours, but this situation might make a difference. We could post a local alert."

Ian nodded. "Where was the car found?" he asked, and Officer McClellan told him.

Then the officer hesitated, waiting for Ian to indicate the action he wanted to take. When Ian made no further comment, he continued, "Well, the car has been towed to the compound. You can claim it whenever you like."

"Thank you."

"Sir, one more thing. If you decide to file a missing-person report, you shouldn't wait too long."

Ian nodded. "I understand."

Ian shut the door behind Officer McClellan and leaned against it with his eyes closed. He clung to the information that there had been no sign of violence.

The small relief that thought carried did not last long. He had started back toward the family room when the telephone rang. He changed direction and went to answer it in the living room.

"Ian Roberts?" the muffled voice on the other end asked, sending a chill down Ian's spine.

"Yes, this is Ian Roberts."

"Listen carefully. If you want to see your wife again, it'll cost you two million dollars. If you doubt what I'm saying, there's an envelope for you in your mailbox. I want the money delivered tomorrow evening. Write this down. I wouldn't want you to get the instructions wrong."

"Wait a minute. I can't raise that much by tomorrow evening. It'll take me at least twenty-four hours to raise that amount of money."

"You wouldn't be trying to stall me, would you?"

"No, no. I'll pay your price, but I want to talk to my wife first."

"Just get the money. And to show my good faith, I'll even throw in the other lady. You're getting two for the price of one." Before Ian could ask any more questions, the other man hung up.

Ian stood there for a few seconds. His worst fears had been realized. He picked up the telephone and dialed Derek's number.

"Hey, Ian, I was just getting ready to call Caroline. Are they back from their shopping trip?"

"No, they're not. Derek, I think you need to come over here," he said. "It's important."

His brother's tone of voice put Derek on guard. "What is it, Ian? What's wrong?"

"I can't discuss it on the phone."

Derek took a deep breath. "I'm on my way."

After he hung up, Ian went to the mailbox, retrieved the envelope, and returned to his den. He scanned the photos with his heart in his throat. How could this have happened? He should have protected her. He slipped the photos back into the envelope and threw it onto the desk.

He then placed a call to Jared Coles, a good friend who was a private investigator. He had been a great help in the past. Ian had no idea if Jared could help him, but it wouldn't hurt to have an ex-policeman around to advise him. He glanced at the envelope on the desk again before going to the family room. His mind had been working, forming plans, since he had heard the kidnapper's demands.

"Liz, can I see you a minute?"

He led her to his den and closed the door. Pacing the room, he shook his head. "I can barely bring myself to say the words."

Liz walked over to him and put her hand on his arm, "What's wrong, Ian?"

He took a deep breath. "Zoe's been kidnapped."

"Oh, my God. You've had a call from the kidnapper?"

Ian rubbed his forehead. "Yes, I've had a call."

"What about Caroline? They were together, weren't they?"

He nodded and closed his eyes. "Yes, they were together. The kidnapper has both of them." He opened his eyes and looked at his sister. "I need your help."

"Anything, Ian. I have some investments I can liquidate. I don't know how much help they'll be, but you're welcome to whatever I have."

Ian turned and hugged her. "Thanks, Liz, but that's not the help I need. I have to get the kids away from here until this is settled. I'll talk to Mom and Dad about taking them to Savannah with them, but I'd like for you to drive. You can take the van."

"Sure, Ian, I'll stay with them, too. I have some vacation time owed to me."

"Thanks, Liz, I'd like for you to leave in the morning."

"Does Derek know?"

"Not yet, he's on his way over. I didn't want to tell him on the phone."

She nodded. "What about Grandma?"

"I'd like to spare her, but I'll leave that decision to Mom and Dad."

"I'll tell Mom and Dad you want to talk to them."

A few minutes later, Ian's parents entered the den. "Liz said you needed to talk to us."

Once they were seated, he explained the situation. "Would you mind taking the kids home with you?"

"Of course, we don't mind. How are you going to explain this to Savannah, though?"

He ran his hand through his hair. "That problem has been in the back of my mind. I'll think of something. I won't tell her until the morning."

His parents looked at each other and nodded. His father was the one to speak up. "Son, you know we have a small nestegg and some investments. You've been very good to us. Whatever you need, just ask."

Ian swallowed hard. He clasped his father's shoulder. "Thanks, Dad, but I can manage that end of it."

At that moment, Derek entered. He looked from his parents to Ian. "What's going on?"

Ian went through his explanation once again. "Mom, Dad, and Liz have agreed to take the kids to Savannah until this is all settled."

His mother stood up. "We'll go and pack." She walked over to Ian and hugged him. Then she turned and hugged Derek. "It'll be all right. We'll be praying for them, for all of you."

"I know, Mom. Thanks for everything."

After their parents had left the room, Derek asked, "Have you called the police?"

"Not yet. Ironically, an officer was here just before I got the call. They found my car double-parked and abandoned at the center. I called Jared, too. He should be here soon. I wanted to talk to him before I call the police. I also want the kids to be away from here first. Once I call the police, it will probably mean involving the FBI." Ian rubbed the back of his neck. "I'm sorry about Caroline, Derek. They weren't after her. She just got caught up in this."

"Ian, you're insulting me. Do you think I'd be any less upset if Caroline weren't involved? Zoe's like a sister to me. You know that."

Ian shook his head. "I know. I guess I'm just not thinking very clearly at the moment."

"I assume you're planning to pay the ransom."

"Yes, but not without a trick up my sleeve. I need your consent, too. If my plan works, we'll recover the ransom money. If it doesn't, losing that amount of money could put the company in serious jeopardy."

"Ian, your designs are mostly responsible for the success of the company."

"We had this discussion before, Derek. You're my partner."

"In that case, whatever you have to do to raise the money is fine with me." He shrugged. "We built one company. If we have to, we can build another. Even if we can't rebuild, I'm sure we agree that losing the company would be nothing compared to losing Zoe and Caroline."

He had barely finished his sentence when the doorbell rang. "That must be Jared," Ian commented. He went to answer the door and returned a few minutes later, followed by Jared.

Ian filled him in on the situation. The three men conferred on a plan of action. Ian suggested planting a tracking device in one of the bundles of money.

Jared nodded. "I agree it's a good plan, Ian."

"I hear a 'but' in there, Jared."

"The 'but' is that you can't do this alone; you need the help of the police. The police may decide to call in the FBI and"—he shook his head—"the FBI does things their way."

"You said the police may call in the FBI. Does that mean FBI involvement isn't a given?"

Jared nodded. "That's right. It'll be up to the Atlanta police to decide whether or not they feel comfortable handling the situation themselves."

"Do you have any idea what they're likely to do?"

"It's hard to tell. With their own SWAT team and hostage negotiator, they may choose not to involve the Feds."

"In that case, do you think they'll go along with this plan?"

"I don't know. All we can do is pitch it to them. It's possible that's the way they would handle it anyway."

"Either way, I won't call anyone until after the kids are away from here. They'll be leaving early in the morning."

About the same time Ian learned of the kidnapping, Zoe and Caroline regained total consciousness. "What are we going to do, Zoe?"

"I don't know. Right now I have a more urgent—although somewhat mundane—need. I have to try to convince whoever's out there to let me use the bathroom."

She started yelling for help. Within seconds, D.C. opened the door, ski mask in place. "You better shut up that noise or I'll stuff your mouth."

"I need to use the bathroom, if there is such a facility in this dump."

D.C. thought about her request for a few seconds. Then he walked over to the mattress and pulled her to her feet. Taking her by the elbow, he pulled her toward the door. He led her down the hall and opened another door.

"Hurry up and don't try nothin'."

Zoe turned her back toward him. "How am I supposed to manage with these?" she asked, indicating the ropes binding her wrists.

D.C. loosed the ropes and she entered the bathroom, closing the door behind her. She looked around the filthy room. She had no choice. Gingerly taking care of her needs, she then turned the water tap. As she expected, nothing happened. She shook her head.

"Oh, well, I suppose a few germs are the least of my worries right now," she muttered to herself.

She opened the door to find D.C. waiting in the hallway. She started back toward the room and he grabbed her elbow.

"Ain't you forgettin' somethin'?" he reminded her, holding up the ropes in front of her face.

"Is that really necessary?"

"I ain't takin' no chances." he insisted, turning her around and binding her wrists again.

He then led her back down the hall. Pushing her ahead of him, he entered the room. He almost lost his patience when Caroline echoed Zoe's request, but he remembered the boss's orders to take good care of them.

When D.C. returned with Caroline, Zoe made another request. "Do you think we could have something to drink? There's no water in the bathroom, not that I'd want to drink from that tap."

D.C. pushed Caroline down on the mattress. "I'll get you a drink."

After their thirsts had been quenched and they were alone once again, Zoe murmured. "Let's try working on these ropes again."

"Even if we get the ropes off, how do you plan to get out of here?" Caroline asked, nodding toward the boarded-up windows.

"I have no idea, but first things first."

# Chapter Eighteen

Ian's second order of business the morning after the kidnapping was to explain her mother's absence to his young daughter. He had already started the ball rolling to raise the funds for the ransom. The story he had devised for Savannah was weak. He was relying heavily on his powers of persuasion and her young age. She was precocious, but she was only five years old, after all.

"Aunt Lizabet said we're going to Grandmom's. Where's Mommy?"

Ian took the child in his lap. "Mommy went to visit a friend, sweetheart."

"She didn't say good-bye."

"No, honey, she didn't have time," he explained, kissing her forehead. "She went to see her friend after she went shopping. Her friend is really sick and Mommy wanted to spend some time with her. You were asleep when she came home to get her things."

Savannah frowned. "Can't I wait for Mommy?"

"I'm afraid not, sweetheart. Mommy won't be back for a few days." He turned her head and lifted her chin. "You like visiting Grandmom and Grandpop, don't you?"

The child bit her lip. "Yeees, but I want to see Mommy."

Ian hugged her close to him. He had known this would not be easy. His daughter had a one-track mind when she wanted something.

"I know, baby, but that's just not possible, right now. You know how you want Mommy with you when you don't feel well. Well, that's how Mommy's friend feels, too."

"Why don't she call her mommy?"

Ian sighed inwardly. This was becoming more complicated than he had bargained for. "She doesn't have a mommy and your mommy is her best friend. Can you be a big girl and do this for Daddy? Please?"

Her answer was a while coming. Finally, she bit her lip and murmured, "Okay."

"Good girl. Now why don't you help Aunt Elizabeth pack your things? You can make sure she has all of your most important toys." He hugged her tightly and kissed her again, before lifting her down from his lap.

Derek entered the den as soon as Savannah left. He had been waiting in the hallway to allow his brother the privacy he needed with his daughter.

Ian sat with his elbows on the desk, his head in his hands. Knowing Caroline was also in the hands of the kidnappers, Derek could imagine some of the emotions running through his brother.

"How did it go?" Derek asked, taking the seat across from him on the other side of the desk. Ian had already told him the story he had prepared for Savannah.

Ian lifted his head and shrugged. "Okay, I guess. At least she didn't cry." He smiled in spite of the circumstances.

"She asked me why Zoe's friend can't call her own mommy to take care of her."

"She'll be fine, Ian. Mom, Dad, and Liz will keep her occupied."

Ian rubbed his eyes. "I know. It's not Savannah I'm worried about. She and Blake will be in good hands and I can't afford to waste any energy worrying about them right now."

Half an hour later, Ian waved good-bye to his children. Jared had arrived a few minutes earlier with Emmett Powell, a friend of his who was now a detective with the Atlanta Police.

The four men adjourned to Ian's den. "Has Jared explained the situation?" Ian asked Emmett.

Jared answered. "No, I wasn't sure you wanted him to know the details yet. You mentioned last night that you wanted to have your children out of the way before the police moved in."

"My wife has been kidnapped," Ian told Emmett. "The car she was driving is in the police compound and I received a call from the kidnapper yesterday evening."

Emmett shook his head. "Ian, I can understand why you wanted to have your children away from here before any action is taken, but you should have called us immediately." Before Ian could reply, he added, "That's beside the point now, though. You said the kidnapper called. What instructions did he give you?"

"He wanted the money delivered this evening. I told him it would take at least twenty-four hours to raise the money. He's calling back tonight. I've already started the process of arranging for the money."

"In that case, I'd better make some calls and get things

set up here. We'll put a tap on your phone, although these days the criminals are usually smart enough not to stay on the phone long enough for a trace. Besides that, if he uses a cell phone he'll probably be long gone from his original location by the time we get a fix on it.''

''I suppose you'll have to involve the FBI?''

''Not unless you feel more comfortable having them handle the investigation. Do you have any reason to believe the kidnapper would have crossed the state line?''

''No,'' Ian replied, rubbing his chin. ''It's odd, but for some reason I have the impression that the kidnapper isn't a total stranger.''

Emmett raised an eyebrow. ''What do you mean?''

''I'm not exactly sure. I guess, for one thing, the fact that Zoe was taken from in front of the center where she volunteers and she happened to be driving my car, not hers. Also, the fact that I've maintained a fairly low profile in the last few years.''

''You may be right, but none of those factors really proves anything,'' Emmett indicated. ''When you come right down to it, I don't think it matters whether the kidnapper is acquainted with you or not.'' He stood up. ''I'd better start making some calls.''

Ian rose from his seat. ''I'll show you to the phone in the other room. It's a separate line and it'll leave this line free in case my accountant calls.''

A few hours later, the police team had arrived and set up operations in Ian's den. Both telephone lines were tapped and a SWAT team was on standby, as well as a hostage negotiator.

It was the second time Ian had heard the SWAT team and hostage negotiator mentioned. He understood the need for having them available, but it did nothing to relieve his fear. In fact, it had the opposite effect.

The accountant had called to update Ian on his efforts to raise the funds. "There's no problem getting the money, Ian. The only problem is the time factor. I'll get back to you as soon as I can."

Cal parked the car at the curb in front of the nearly deserted building for what he planned to be the last time. Once he had picked up the money, he had no intention of returning to pay off the two nitwits upstairs.

He knocked on the door and it was opened immediately by D.C. "Is everything quiet?"

"Yeah, sure, after they screamed their heads off when they woke up. They shut up when I threatened to gag 'em. Said they was only wantin' to use the john. Not that any of those people out there would come to help 'em. They asked for some water and I gave it to 'em."

"You were careful to wear the ski masks, weren't you?"

"You know, man," D.C. said, waving his arms, "JoJo's right. You act like we stupid or somethin'. You think we wanna be fingered? Yeah, I wore the mask."

"As you're so fond of saying, chill, man. I'm just checking to make sure my instructions have been followed."

"When we gonna get our dough?"

"The drop is tomorrow," Cal informed him, walking toward the back room. Before entering, he put on his own ski mask and picked up one of the lamps.

Caroline and Zoe lay in the same positions he had first seen them. They looked at the two men, trying very hard not to reveal their fear. Their efforts were unsuccessful.

"There's no reason to be afraid, ladies. As soon as I have my money, your families will be told where to find you."

He took out his cell phone and dialed Ian's number. Ian answered after the first ring.

"You wanted to talk to your wife," Cal said tersely. He held the phone up to Zoe's ear.

"Ian?"

"Are you all right, baby?"

"Yes, they haven't hurt us."

Before she could say another word, Cal snatched the phone back. "That's enough. I'll call you tomorrow with the instructions."

"I want to talk to my wife again before the drop."

Cal made no reply. "You'll be told where to find them after I'm well away from here." He hung up the phone and left the room.

When they were alone, Caroline whispered, "We have to get these ropes off, Zoe. I don't trust that they'll release us."

"Turn around. I'll take another stab at it. I thought I had managed to loosen them a little before."


The bank officer arrived with the money just before one o'clock on Sunday. "I trust I can count on your complete secrecy, Mr. Brannigan," Ian commented as he signed the papers.

"Of course, Mr. Roberts." He handed over the suitcase and extended his hand. "Good luck, Mr. Roberts."

Ian took the hand extended to him. "Thank you, and thank you for spending your weekend taking care of this matter."

Brannigan shook his head. "There's no need to thank me for that, Mr. Roberts. Under the circumstances, I could hardly refuse."

After Brannigan left, Emmett prepared the money. A tracking device was placed inside the band of one of the bundles of money. "We can keep a discrete distance and still follow the signal."

The same question was running through the minds of Ian and Emmett, but neither voiced it. What if the men did not return to where the women were being held? There was no assurance that they would not simply take off to parts unknown.

If that happened, the police could apprehend them, but would they tell them where they had been holding Caroline and Zoe? And depending on where they were being held, locating them might involve some urgency.

The kidnapper had complied with Ian's request to speak with Zoe when he called with the new instructions. Ian only had time to hear her voice before he was cut off.

Ian arrived at the first site the kidnapper had given him. A few minutes later the pay telephone rang, as he had been told to expect. This procedure was followed several more times, sending him from one location to another via pay telephones. He was finally given the name of a restaurant. His instructions were to leave the money in a specific stall in the restroom.

Unknown to him, Cal was waiting in the restaurant, having left D.C. outside in the car. He was careful to request a table near the rear of the room, but within sight of the front door and the alcove where the restrooms were located.

Cal watched from behind the menu as Ian entered the restaurant. Ian scanned the main room of the restaurant before walking over to the alcove and entering the restroom.

The room was empty. Ian walked over to the stall and

took a deep breath. He opened the door, put the duffle bag on the seat, and quickly left the room.

Keeping an eye on the restroom to be sure no one else exited with the duffle bag, Cal waited until Ian left the restaurant before placing some bills on the table and walking toward the restroom. He entered and checked the room to be sure that there were no other occupants. Then he walked over and removed the "Out of Order" sign from the stall.

He closed the door to the stall and took the jogging suit and running shoes from his own duffle bag. After changing his clothes, he transferred the money from Ian's bag to his. Leaving Ian's bag in the stall, he left the restroom. He then calmly left the restaurant.

Cal took a quick look around and then hurried to the side street, where he had parked his car. He opened the door of the car, threw the duffle bag in the back seat, got into the driver's seat, and drove off.

D.C. grinned. "We did it, man!" D.C. said. He was almost jumping up and down in his seat.

A few minutes later, after he had calmed down, D.C. glanced at Cal. "Hey man, you really gonna let the chicks go?"

"Yeah, I'll let them go. They don't know anything and I plan to be long gone by the time I call to let them know where to find them. I told you I wouldn't ask you to kill anyone, didn't I?"

D.C. nodded. Fifty thousand dollars would take him a long way from Atlanta.


The police had followed Ian from a distance. When they saw him leave the restaurant empty-handed, they waited a few minutes to be sure no one was following him. Ian walked to the next block, where they picked him up. Jared got out of the police car and Ian handed him his car keys. Jared would drive Ian's car back to the house while Ian accompanied the police as they tracked the kidnapper.

# Chapter Nineteen

By the time Ian was ready to leave the house to make the drop, Zoe had managed to loosen Caroline's ropes enough for her to slip her hands out. It took a few minutes for Caroline to free her friend and a few more for them to get the circulation in their hands completely restored.

"Now what?" Caroline asked.

"I guess we should try to find out how many of them are out there? We know there are at least two. The one who made the call to Ian must have gone to pick up the money. There must have been two of them who grabbed us at the center," Zoe suggested. "We don't know if the one who made the call was one of them at the center."

She picked up the rope that had bound her hands. "Get yours. If it sounds like they're coming back, we'll have to get back in our positions and hope they don't actually check the ropes."

They listened at the door and were pleased with the con-

versation they overheard. As Zoe expected, the man with
the phone was telling someone that he was leaving to pick
up the money.

"We're goin' with you," JoJo insisted.

Cal shook his head. "And who do you think is going to
stay here and guard those two in there?"

"That ain't my problem no more. What's to keep you
from runnin' off with our share?"

Ian clenched his teeth. It appeared he had underestimated
his helpers. No matter, a hundred thousand dollars out of
two million was a small price to pay.

"Okay, okay. D.C., you come with me." He looked at
JoJo. "You trust your friend, don't you?"

"Yeah, yeah, I trust D.C."

"Fine, let's go."

When Zoe and Caroline heard the door close, they looked
at each other. "At least the odds are in our favor now,"
Zoe said.

"That's great, but how do we get out of here?"

They looked around the dim room. Even if there was a
fire escape, the boarded-up window provided no exit. The
only furniture other than the mattress was a dilapidated
wooden chair.

"I have an idea," Caroline said. "He came in before,
when we were screaming. If we start screaming and banging
on the window boards, he'll come in again."

"And then what?"

"I'll stand behind the door and when he comes in, I'll
hit him with the chair. Between the two of us, we should
be able to overpower him. I haven't seen any of them with
a gun, so we have a chance."

Zoe bit her lip. "I don't know, Caroline. It sounds good,
but I've been accused of being impulsive my whole life.
Maybe both of us have been watching too much television.

Even though we haven't seen a gun it doesn't mean he's unarmed.''

"Do you have a better idea?''

Zoe shook her head. "No.''

"Do you agree that we can't just wait here and count on their promise to let us go after they have the money?''

"All right, you've made your point. Let's give it a shot.''

Caroline positioned herself behind the door and nodded to Zoe. Just as they suspected, Caroline heard the man unlock the door almost as soon as Zoe began screaming. He burst through the door and looked at the mattress.

In the split second before his mind registered the fact that the women were no longer lying on it, Caroline swung the chair with the full force of her body behind it. The chair broke apart when it came in contact with JoJo's body and he fell to his knees.

That was not enough for Caroline. She brought what was left of the chair down on his head and he stretched out on the floor. She raised the remnants of wood again, but Zoe stopped her.

"I think he's out, Caroline. Let's get out of here before the others come back.''

They fled the room and raced down the stairs. It was dusk when they exited the building. In their haste, Caroline tripped and tumbled down the stone stairs.

"Oh God, Caroline," Zoe cried as she went to help her up. "Are you all right?''

Stunned, Caroline tried to stand. The stabbing pain in her side made it difficult to talk. "I think so.''

She winced when she got to her feet. "I think I sprained my ankle." She shook her head in disgust. "Isn't that typical? In the movies, every time a woman is running away from danger, she trips and sprains her ankle.''

"Put your arm around my shoulder. We have to get off the street before they come back."

With Zoe supporting Caroline, the women made it to a nearby alley. When they emerged on the next street over, Caroline urged Zoe to stop. Every breath was like a stab in her side.

"I can't do it, Zoe. You'll have to go for help."

Zoe shook her head. "I can't leave you here alone, Caroline. What if they come back and start looking for you?"

"I don't think they will. They'll probably be more interested in getting as far away as possible after they get the money."

She looked around the alley. "It's almost dark. I'll hide over there by that doorway and you can come back when you get help."

Zoe forced back the tears that had been threatening for two days. They were too close to give up now. "I can't leave you. I'll just wait here with you until you catch your breath."

Caroline shook her head. "It's not just having the wind knocked out of me, it's the pain. Please, Zoe. You have to leave me here and get help."

"All right, all right." She helped Caroline over to the doorway. "I'll be back soon. I promise."


Ian and Derek sat in the back of the unmarked police car.

Emmett had balked when Ian requested to accompany the police as they tracked the kidnapper after the ransom drop. He finally relented, but he had insisted they ride in another car behind him.

\*   \*   \*

Zoe had only gone a few yards beyond the alley when Ian spied her from the unmarked police car. "Officer Holmes, stop the car."

"What?"

"Stop the car. That's my wife over there."

The officer had barely pulled the car over to the curb before Ian was out and sprinting across the street, calling Zoe's name. She turned around and stood frozen to the spot for a few seconds, then she was running toward him.

"Ian? How did you find me? Never mind—it doesn't matter. We have to help Caroline."

Derek was right behind Ian. "Where's Caroline? Do they still have her?"

"No, we escaped."

Officer Holmes heard her comment as he approached. "Mr. Roberts, I'll radio Detective Powell that we have the women." He left the three of them and returned to the car.

"Caroline fell and sprained her ankle, Ian."

"Where is she?"

"In the alley. She said she couldn't go any farther," she explained as she led Ian and Derek through the alley. Derek was the first to spot Caroline huddled in the doorway.

She looked up when he called her name and started running toward her. She gasped in pain when he scooped her up in his arms.

"What is it, baby? Zoe said you sprained your ankle."

"I don't know. I fell down the stairs. My side hurts. Oh, Derek, I'm so glad to see you."

Officer Holmes had driven the car around to the other side of the street and stopped in front of the alley. He got out of the car just as Derek reached the street with Caroline in his arms.

"Is she badly hurt?" Should I call an ambulance?"

Derek had heard her labored breathing as he carried her.

"Yes, she has a sprained ankle, but I think there may be more than that wrong with her."

Caroline shook her head. "No, Derek, I don't need an ambulance. We can probably get to the hospital faster by going in the car than waiting for an ambulance."

Derek looked at the officer. "Call the ambulance."

The ambulance arrived within ten minutes and Caroline was on her way to the hospital, accompanied by Derek. Zoe insisted on following them to see for herself that her friend was not seriously injured.

Although Zoe had insisted she was unhurt, the nurse had suggested that it would be wise to allow the doctor to examine her. Other than being exhausted and slightly dehydrated, she was pronounced fit and released. The nurse and Ian had been pumping her with liquids since the doctor made his pronouncement.

Ian hugged his wife close to his side as they waited to hear the doctor's verdict on Caroline's condition. Once again, he was amazed at Zoe's strength. With all that she had been through in the past two days, his wife was incredibly calm.

Derek paced the floor. Finally, the doctor entered the waiting room. "Mr. Derek Roberts?" he asked, looking from Derek to Ian.

As Ian turned toward his brother, Derek answered, "Yes?"

"In the absence of family, Ms. Duval indicated I should speak to you."

"How is she?"

"She said she fell down a flight of stone stairs."

Derek nodded.

"She's very lucky. She has a few bruised ribs and a badly sprained ankle. There's no concussion and she doesn't appear to have any internal injuries. We'd like to keep her overnight for observation to rule out that possibility, though."

"May I see her?"

"Certainly, although she's not very lucid. The bruised ribs are quite painful. We've given her something to alleviate it."

Caroline's eyes were closed when Derek entered the small cubicle. Her eyelids fluttered when he spoke her name.

Taking her hand in his, he kissed the palm. "How are you feeling, sweetheart?"

She gave him a half smile. "I'm not sure, but other than the pain, I think I felt better before I came here. At least I had my mental faculties then. Right now, my mind feels mushy."

Derek smiled. "That's the pain medication."

"How's Zoe?"

"Zoe's fine. She's worried about you. Would you like to see her?"

She nodded and he left the cubicle. Zoe entered a moment later with Ian following behind her. She hugged Caroline, gently.

"We make quite a team, girlfriend. I don't think I'd have been able to manage without you."

Caroline gave her the same drowsy smile she had given Derek. "From what I've heard, you manage pretty well on your own. As crazy as it sounds, though, I'm glad we were together. It wasn't nearly as scary as being alone." Her voice trailed off at the end of the sentence.

"I think we'd better leave you now," Derek suggested. "You need to rest. They'll be moving you to a room soon."

They left her and returned to the waiting area. "I'm going to stay here, Ian."

Ian nodded, hugging Zoe close to his side. "I'd better take my wife home before she falls flat on her face from exhaustion. The police officer said he'd wait for us outside."

The three of them hugged and Ian urged Zoe toward the door.

Zoe could barely stand by the time the police car dropped them off at home. Ian helped her out of the car and up the walkway. As they entered the house, Zoe was struck by the silence. She looked around.

"Where is everyone?"

"I sent the kids to Savannah with Mom, Dad, and Liz," He explained, helping off with her coat.

She turned and looked up into her husband's face. For the first time since she had run into his arms that evening, she saw the weariness in his eyes.

"I didn't know what to expect," he said.

She reached up and caressed his cheek. "I understand," she whispered.

"I'll call Mom and Dad as soon as I get you settled." He lifted her in his arms and carried her up the stairs.

"I need to take a shower, Ian," she said when he set her on her feet.

"Honey, you can barely stand. How about a nice bath instead?"

Zoe nodded. "Maybe you're right. A nice hot bath sounds great."

She sat on the vanity stool while he ran the bath water. She started to undress, but she had difficulty making her fingers work to unbutton her blouse.

While the water filled the tub, Ian helped her undress. A few minutes later, he helped her into the tub.

"You just sit here and relax. Aside from the bath, you need to eat something." He smiled. "How about a leftover turkey sandwich?"

"Since I haven't had a chance to get tired of turkey, that sounds good."

Ian had not returned when Zoe was ready to get out of the tub. With some effort, she dragged herself up and stepped out of the water. She wrapped the towel around herself, but could manage no more. Her reserves of strength and energy exhausted, she slumped to the floor, sobbing.

Before preparing her snack, Ian dialed his parents' number. His mother answered with the second ring.

"Hi, Mom. We have Zoe and Caroline. They're both safe."

His mother sighed. "Thank God. Were they hurt?"

"Not by the kidnappers. Caroline fell down the stairs when they were escaping, but she just has a few minor injuries."

"They escaped?"

"That's right. It seems Zoe's found a kindred spirit in Caroline. Neither one of them is what would be called a shrinking violet."

"In this case, that trait served them well. You'd better go now, son. You must be exhausted. I'll give the others the good news, but I don't think I'd better mention to your daughter that her mother is at home."

"You're right. Don't tell her anything until you're ready to leave to bring them home."

"We'll call you tomorrow. Give Zoe our love."

"I'll do that."

Ian returned to the bedroom a few minutes later and was surprised by the sounds coming from the bathroom. He set the tray on a table and hurried to his wife. Lifting her to her feet, he snatched his own thick terry robe from the hook beside the tub and wrapped her in it.

Carrying her to the bedroom, he sat down in the armchair with her on his lap. She shivered in his arms and he pulled the afghan from the back of the chair and tucked it around her.

"It's all right, baby. You're safe now."

"It's all my fault, Ian," she murmured through her sobs. "Caroline had nothing to do with this. They didn't want her. They wanted me. Now she's hurt and it's all my fault."

Ian tightened his arms around her and kissed her temple. "No, sweetheart, it's not your fault. It's the kidnappers' fault. Caroline will be fine and you heard what she said. She was glad you didn't have to go through that experience alone."

"I was so scared. I didn't want to leave her alone."

"But you did the right thing. If you hadn't left her to look for help, we wouldn't have seen you. Right?"

Zoe nodded against his chest. "Right."

"The important thing is that you're both safe now."

Moments later, her soft, even breathing told him she had fallen asleep. He knew he should carry her to the bed, but he could not bring himself to let her go, even for a few minutes. He just wanted to hold her for a while and savor the feeling of having her safe in his arms again.

Finally, he removed the afghan and robe and carried her to bed. After undressing, he lay down beside her and pulled her into his arms again. The restless nights caught up with him and soon he, too, drifted off to sleep.

# Chapter Twenty

Late the next morning, Zoe awoke alone in bed. She stretched and sat up. Retrieving her robe from the foot of the bed, she slipped her arms into the sleeves and padded to the bathroom. A few minutes later, she made her way down the stairs, following the aroma of freshly brewed coffee. Ian was standing at the stove clad in his robe. He sensed her presence and turned his attention from the bacon frying on the stove.

"Good morning," he said, pulling the pan from the stove and setting it aside.

They met in the middle of the room, wrapping their arms around each other. Their lips met in a warm, sweet kiss.

"Good morning," Zoe whispered.

"How are you feeling?" he asked, pulling her closer.

"Blessed. Very, very blessed," she murmured, resting her head against his chest.

Ian sighed. "That makes two of us."

"Have you heard from Derek?"

Ian shook his head. "I know he was planning to remain at the hospital. I'm sure if there had been any change in Caroline, he would have called."

"What about the kids?"

"I called Mom last night and told her the news. She said she'd call back today."

He leaned back a few inches and she looked up into eyes filled with all the love anyone could ever wish. "You ruined my surprise," he chastised.

"What surprise?"

"I was planning to bring you breakfast in bed."

"Well, it doesn't have to be ruined." She eased from his embrace and walked over to one of the cabinets.

"You fix the plates and I'll get the trays. We'll just carry everything upstairs."

A short time later, Zoe was sitting up in bed with the tray across her lap. Ian sat facing her on the side of the bed. They fed each other tidbits of bacon, French toast, and melon. When Ian placed the last piece of melon in Zoe's mouth, she closed her lips around his fingers and began gently sucking them.

Ian lifted her hand from where it rested on the bed, turned it over and planted a kiss in the center of her palm. Then he began slowly drawing circles in it with his tongue. From there, he worked his way slowly up her arm.

Gently pulling his hand from her mouth, Ian suggested, "I think we'd better put this tray out of the way. What do you think?"

"I think that might be wise."

After he set the tray on the table across the room, Ian returned to his seat on the side of the bed. "Now, where were we?"

"I think you had decided that it would be nice to have dessert after breakfast."

Ian grinned. "Exactly," he agreed, loosening the tie belt of her robe and slipping it off her shoulders.

Zoe rose to her knees and flung the robe to the foot of the bed. "Your turn."

Ian quickly disposed of his own robe. He stood at the side of the bed and reached out, pulling her toward him and inhaling her seductive fragrance. His arms encircled her, his shaft pressing against the silky pelt at the juncture of her thighs.

The muscles in his lower abdomen tightened when her hands clasped his buttocks. She planted kisses on his shoulder in a prelude to her tongue slowly licking a moist trail across his collarbone and up the side of his neck. The spicy scent emanating from his skin engulfed her.

Ian's hands slid slowly up and down her back before coming to rest on her derriere. His knee slid between her legs and she gasped when his fingers probed the slippery, satiny skin beneath the triangle of hair.

"Oh my sweet, sweet Zoe," he murmured in her ear. One hand continued to stroke the sensitive place that pulsed with need. The other hand covered her breast, his thumb stroking the already stiff nipple.

Zoe's hand slid between their bodies to play in the mat of hair surrounding his shaft. Then her fingers gently stroked the soft skin of his rigid member.

When Ian could stand the torture no longer, he eased her onto her back. He entered her in one long swift movement and she wrapped her legs tightly around his waist. They moved together as they had so many times before, but somehow different than ever before. It was a celebration of life and love.

She cried out his name in ecstasy. Ian's cries of pleasure

followed seconds later. He collapsed on top of her. When he attempted to move, her arms tightened around him.

"Don't leave me."

He kissed her tenderly. "Never, baby, but I'm too heavy for you."

She sighed. "It feels good."

Ian chuckled and rolled over, pulling her to lie on top of him. "That's better."

Pulling the covers over them, he wrapped his arms around her again. Minutes later, they were both asleep.


That same afternoon, Derek had another conversation with Caroline's doctor. She had had a restless night. Although she had opened her eyes a few times, she had never fully awakened.

"I don't understand, Dr. Jensen. You said there were no serious injuries. Why do you want to keep her another night?"

"I said there didn't appear to be any serious injuries. I still believe that's the case, but she was running a fever last night. There could be a number of reasons for that. As I mentioned before, she's slightly dehydrated. That could contribute to the fever. There's a chance that the emotional trauma itself might play a role in it. We're running some more tests to rule out any possibility of infection."

Derek ran his hand through his hair. "Is it normal for her to sleep so long?"

"I wouldn't be concerned about that. The exhaustion and the pain medication would account for that. She may sleep straight through for another twelve hours or more."

Derek nodded. "You expect she'll be discharged tomorrow, though?"

"Right now, I believe that's likely. As I said, we are

running a few tests and we'll see what happens tonight with her temperature.''

After his conversation with the doctor, Derek called Ian and Zoe and filled them in. "I called Caroline's parents last night. I thought it best not to tell them anything about the kidnapping. I explained that she had fallen down a flight of stairs and told them the extent of her injuries. I thought I'd better let them know so they can contact the school."

"Did they buy your explanation?''

"I think so. I said that she was unable to talk on the phone because of the pain medication, and that I would have her call them as soon as she's able. That should be tomorrow at the latest."

"Have you been at the hospital all this time?''

"I went home and showered and changed this morning. Other than that, yes, I've been here the whole time. I plan to be here until she wakes up. The nurse tried to kick me out last night, but Dr. Jensen stepped in and okayed my being here."

"I'll give Zoe the news. Keep us posted."

"How is Zoe?''

"I think she's a little more shaken than she wants to admit. She broke down last night; probably a delayed reaction. She's strong, though. She'll be fine."

"What about the kids?''

"I talked to Liz. She and Dad are driving them home tomorrow. I tried to talk them into flying, but she insisted they can handle it and Dad wants to pick up his own car."

"I'll let you go now. I'll probably see you tomorrow."


Later that afternoon, Ian had a visit from Jared. Zoe was in the kitchen preparing dinner while Ian attempted to catch up on his work. He ushered Jared into the den.

"What's the news?" he asked, taking his seat behind the desk.

Jared sat down across from him. "They caught all of the kidnappers. They also recovered the ransom money. Emmett will be in touch with you about that."

Ian raised an eyebrow. "I get the feeling there's something you're not telling me."

"Did you know that Cal was released from prison six months ago?"

Ian frowned. "Cal?"

Jared nodded.

Ian grasped the edge of the desk with both hands. "Are you telling me that Cal is behind the kidnapping?" he asked through clenched teeth.

Jared nodded again. "He hired the other two for the actual kidnapping, but he was behind it all."

Ian stood up and began pacing. "That little stunt he pulled six years ago wasn't bad enough? He actually kidnapped my wife?"

Jared made no comment. He had been involved in Cal's prior arrest. He knew Ian well enough to know that what Cal had done years earlier was nothing compared to his latest crime.

Ian stopped pacing, took a deep breath and sat back down in his chair. He closed his eyes, shaking his head.

"So, a few years in a minimum security facility wasn't enough for him. Now he'll spend the rest of his life in a real prison, a maximum security prison."

Jared cleared his throat. "Not exactly."

Ian opened his eyes at that statement. "What does that mean?" He shook his head. "Don't tell me he's going to get away with this, Jared."

"No, he's not going to get away with it. He exacted his own punishment."

Ian leaned forward. "What do you mean?"

"When the police cornered him, he was armed. When he saw that there was no escape, he turned the gun on himself."

Ian closed his eyes, covering his face with his hands. "Oh, God. He deserved to be punished, but . . ." He shook his head. "It may sound terrible to say, but I'm glad his mother's not alive to see what he'd become."

"I'm sorry, Ian."

"Thanks, Jared, I'm sorry, too. I'm sorry he never seemed to get his life on the right track."


On Tuesday morning, Derek was once again parked at Caroline's bedside. He had left the hospital for two hours the previous evening. The nurse informed him that Caroline had awakened slightly for about half an hour while he was gone. She was asleep again when he returned to the hospital and she had slept through the night.

Just after nine o'clock, Derek's pager went off. He looked at the telephone number and left the room to call the office.

"What's up, Keisha?"

"I'm really sorry to bother you, Derek. Ian called me yesterday and told me what had happened. How's Caroline?"

"She'll be fine. The doctor originally planned to keep her overnight, but decided to keep her an extra day. They've run tests and there doesn't seem to be any serious injury. Is that why you called?"

Keisha sighed. "I'm afraid not. Tyrone's having a problem with the job at the DMV. He thinks there may be a virus in the system. He got out and closed it down, but I think it requires some hands-on from someone a little more experienced. I'm tied up here and I don't have anyone else to send. I haven't called Ian yet . . ."

Derek cut in. "No, no, don't bother Ian. Elizabeth is bringing the kids home today. He has enough on his plate right now. I'll go over to the DMV and see what I can do."

"Thanks. I'll let Tyrone know that you're on your way."

Derek pocketed his cell phone and returned to Caroline's room. She was still asleep. He walked across the hall to the nurses' station.

"Excuse me, I'm sorry to bother you. Could I have a blank sheet of paper?"

Paper in hand, he returned again to Caroline's room. He wrote a short note, folded it, and laid it on the bedside table. Then he leaned over and kissed her cheek before quietly exiting, closing the door behind him.


Caroline was still asleep when the nurse entered fifteen minutes later to freshen her pitcher of water. She awakened as the nurse was leaving the room.

The pain in her ankle had eased, but every breath reminded her of the bruised ribs. She looked around the room, frowning. Several times in the last two days when she had awakened, she thought she saw Derek in the room. She sighed. It must have been a dream.

She swung her legs over the side of the bed and reached for the crutches. A few minutes later, she exited the bathroom just as the doctor entered the room.

After examining her, he made a few notes on her chart. "I'm glad to see your temperature is normal. We've run a few tests and I have some good news. There's no sign of any infection. The sprained ankle and a few badly bruised ribs are the extent of your injuries.

"I'm discharging you, but you should take it easy. I suggest that you see your family doctor within the next few days. Ice packs should help relieve the pain in your side and the swelling in your ankle. I'm also leaving a prescription for the pain.''

''Thank you.''

He left the room. The nurse started to follow him, but Caroline called her back. ''Is anyone waiting to see me?''

''No, I just came on duty, but there were no visitors out there. It's too early for visiting hours.''

Caroline nodded and mumbled her thanks. After the nurse left the room, she picked up the phone. Her first inclination was to call Derek, but she changed her mind. He must be having second thoughts about their relationship.

She had no idea what it had cost Ian to ransom her from the kidnappers. Whatever they had demanded for Zoe was probably increased by Caroline's presence. Ian could hardly agree to ransom his wife and not ransom her friend.

They had all seem concerned about her, but that was before they had time to consider the financial consequences. Caroline had no idea of the severity of those consequences nor the discord it may have caused between Derek and Ian.

Vanessa should be at work by now. She dialed her friend's work number. Vanessa asked about her injuries and Caroline assured her she was fine.

''I need a favor, Vanessa. Can you take off for a few hours?''

''Probably. What's up?''

''I'm being discharged and I need some clothes.''

''You want me to bring you a change of clothes?''

''Yes, I know that I'm asking a lot to ask you to leave work and come here.''

''It's not a problem, Caroline.''

''There's more, Vanessa. I'd like for you to get all of my things from Zoe's house. I'm leaving today.''

''Caroline, you already told me you're being discharged.

Have you decided to come and stay with me for a few days?''

"No, I'm going home. My airline ticket was for Sunday, but I should be able to get a seat on today's flight. I'll call the airline as soon as I hang up.''

"What if there's no room on the flight?''

"Then I'll wait another day. That is, if you'll let me stay with you until then.''

"Of course, you can stay with me. In fact, I think you should stay with me for a few days. I don't think traveling this soon is a good idea.''

"Vanessa, please, will you just get my things and bring them here? And don't tell Zoe I'm leaving Atlanta today.''

Vanessa sighed. There was more happening than her friend was admitting. Whatever it was, it was obvious she intended to keep it to herself.

"I'll be there as soon as I can.''


Vanessa felt a little uncomfortable with Caroline's request to keep her departure a secret. She had been unable to leave work immediately and it was past noon when she arrived at Zoe's house. Ian answered the door and Vanessa could hear Savannah's voice in the background.

"Hi, Ian. I hope I'm not interrupting anything. Caroline asked me to pick up her things. She's being discharged from the hospital today.''

"She's not planning to come here?''

"No, I guess she thought it might be best to give you and Zoe some time alone.''

"I see,'' he replied, nodding his head slowly. "I'll show you to her room.''

He led the way up the stairs. They reached the room and he pointed to the closet.

"Her luggage should be in there and any clothes in the closet or the drawers belongs to her. The police returned her purse, too. It was still in the car and the contents appeared to be intact. It's hanging on the hook in the closet."

Vanessa nodded and retrieved the luggage from the closet. She looked through the clothes on the hanger, trying to decide on a comfortable outfit for the flight.

"I'll leave you to pack," Ian said. "Let me know when you're ready and I'll take the bags down."

A while later, Ian watched Vanessa drive away. He had told Zoe about her visit and her request. They both assumed Caroline had planned to spend the next few days with her friend. Ian wondered that Derek had not called to inform him of this change in Caroline's plans. He had heard nothing from his brother that morning, and he and Zoe had been busy with getting the children settled.

Vanessa arrived at the hospital less than two hours after leaving work. Caroline was seated on the side of the bed.

"I left your suitcase in the car," Vanessa explained, holding up a bag. "There's a change of clothes in here. You have your coat with you, don't you?"

"Yes, I checked with the nurse. It's in the closet with my other clothes."

She emptied the bag. "I was able to get a seat on this afternoon's flight. I called my parents and they'll meet me at the airport."

"Oh, I have your purse in my car. It was still on the seat when the police recovered Zoe's car."

"Great. Could you hand me those crutches, please? I'd better get dressed."

"Do you need any help?"

"No, thanks. The nurse took the bandages off just before you arrived. She said to call her and she'll redo them after I take a quick shower."

Sometime later, Caroline was settled in Vanessa's car and on her way to the airport. Vanessa had made no further attempt to dissuade her from leaving Atlanta that day.

"Aren't you going to say good-bye to everyone?"

"I'll call Zoe when I get home."

Vanessa glanced at her friend. The fact that she made no mention of Derek was a glaring omission. She wondered, again, what had happened between them. It seemed that that old saying was right, the path to true love never ran smoothly.

Later that afternoon, Caroline was on a plane headed for Connecticut. A tear slid down her cheek as she watched the landscape of Georgia disappear.

"Good-bye, Derek," she whispered.

# Chapter Twenty-one

Derek returned to the hospital that evening. He went directly to Caroline's room, opened the door, and stopped abruptly in his tracks. A nurses' aide was remaking the bed and Caroline was nowhere in sight. He should have called ahead. Dr. Jensen had said she would probably be discharged that day.

"Excuse me, has Miss Duval been discharged?"

"I think so. I was told to make up the room for a new patient they're sending up from Emergency."

Derek started to turn away and she called him back. "I think your friend left this behind," she said, holding up his note. "I found it under the bed. I don't know if it's important, but would you see that she gets it?"

Derek took the note, fingering it absently in his hand. "You said you found it on the floor?"

"That's right. Under the bed."

"Thank you, yes, I'll see that she gets it."

After he was settled in his car, Derek called Ian. Zoe answered the phone. "Hi, Zoe. How are you feeling? Did Liz and the kids arrive?"

"I'm fine, Derek, and yes, the kids are here. My daughter has been lecturing me all day about leaving without telling her good-bye."

"Well, it sounds like everything is back to normal."

"Yes, very much so. Did you want to speak to Ian?"

"As a matter of fact, I called to speak to Caroline."

"She's not here. Vanessa came and picked up her things this afternoon. I thought that was a little strange when Ian told me. I expected you to be at the hospital when she was discharged. I guess she decided to stay with Vanessa for a few days."

"Okay, thanks, Zoe. Take care of yourself and kiss the kids for me."

"I will."

Derek hung up and dialed Vanessa's number. He greeted Caroline's friend briefly when she answered.

"May I speak to Caroline, Vanessa?"

Derek had a sinking feeling in his stomach when there was no response for a few seconds following his question. "Vanessa?"

Vanessa sighed. "She's not here, Derek. I took her to the airport this afternoon. She caught a plane back to Connecticut."

One word echoed through Derek's mind. *Why?* There was no point in voicing that question to Vanessa. He had learned his lesson the hard way. Never again would he look for explanations for Caroline's behavior from a third party. He would get the answer directly from Caroline, in person.

\* \* \*

The next morning, Derek stopped by his brother's house. "Hi, Ian. I just came by to tell you I'm flying to Connecticut this afternoon."

"You're taking Caroline home?"

Derek rubbed his neck. "No, Caroline's already at home."

Ian frowned. "I thought something was a little strange when Vanessa came to pick up her belongings. Vanessa mentioned that Caroline felt she should give Zoe and me some time alone and we assumed she was planning to stay with Vanessa for a few days. I don't understand what's going on."

Derek shook his head. "Neither do I."

"You weren't at the hospital when she was discharged?"

Derek shook his head. "I left the hospital early yesterday morning to help Tyrone with a problem at the DMV. I didn't get back until evening and she was gone."

"How was she when you left?"

"I never really had a chance to talk to her. She was asleep most of the time that I was at the hospital. She opened her eyes a few times, but she wasn't really awake. I don't think she was even aware that I was there."

Ian looked down at the floor. "Do you think she blamed us somehow for involving her in this whole affair?"

"Ian, I think Caroline would be insulted that you'd even consider that possibility. No, I don't think her abrupt departure had anything to do with you."

He ran his hand through his hair. "The nearest I can figure it is that she never knew I was there and she thought I had deserted her. After all we've been through, I can't believe she'd think that, but I can't come up with any other explanation. I left a note, but I'm not sure she ever saw it. I have to go to Connecticut and talk to her, Ian. A telephone call won't do. I need to see her."

Ian nodded. "I talked to Keisha today and she told me

about calling you to help Tyrone, but I had no idea it was an all-day job. Thanks. If your absence from the hospital had anything to do with Caroline leaving Atlanta so quickly, I'm sorry. Do whatever you feel you have to do to make it right, Derek. We'll manage here.''

While Derek was boarding his flight, Ian was listening to the minister's final words at Cal's graveside ceremony. In spite of all that had happened, he and his parents had felt the need to pay their final respects. Ian's main reason for coming had been to lend support to Sharmane. She, too, had suffered a great deal from Cal's actions.

He watched her closely. He also watched the man who had been at her side since they entered the church earlier that day. Ian had had no opportunity to speak with them, but the man's obvious care and concern for Sharmane had piqued his interest.

When the service had ended, the few friends that were present dispersed, stopping to offer words of sympathy before returning to their cars. Ian followed his parents as they approached Sharmane. A moment later he was face to face with the woman he had once planned to marry. It seemed now that centuries had passed since that time.

After performing the introductions, Sharmane murmured, ''I was surprised to see you in church. Thank you for coming.''

Ian shrugged. ''It just seemed the right thing to do.''

Sharmane cleared her throat. ''Ian, I'm sorry. I read in the paper what Cal had done. I never would have expected him to do anything so awful. If I had had any idea . . .''

Ian stopped her. ''Sharmane, you don't need to apologize for Cal's actions. He made his choices. It had nothing to do with you. The truth is, you're probably the best thing that

ever happened to him. It's just sad that he never managed
to get his life on the right track."

She nodded. She had done all she could to help Cal, but
it was never enough.

Ian took her hand in his. "Take care of yourself and
please let me know if there's anything I can do to help."

"Thanks, but I'll be fine," she assured him.

Ian met Jeff's gaze and the corner of his mouth lifted
slightly. He nodded and Jeff returned the gesture. Yes, Sharmane would be all right. Today had closed another chapter
in both of their lives.


Derek landed in Hartford late that afternoon. He picked
up the rental car and drove directly to Caroline's house. As
he drove, the possibility occurred to him that she might have
gone to stay with her parents for a few days. If that was the
case, he would simply follow her there.

He parked at the curb in front of her house, got out of
the car, and walked slowly to the door. He took a deep
breath before ringing the bell. It was opened by Caroline's
father.

"Hello, Mr. Duval. I'm here to see Caroline."

"Well, young man, come in. Caroline didn't tell us you
were coming. It's good to see you again."

Grace entered the hallway just as he finished his sentence.

"Derek, how nice of you to come all this way to see
Caroline. She didn't tell us you were coming."

"Hello, Mrs. Duval, it's good to see you again, too. Actually, Caroline didn't know I was planning to come. Where
is she?"

"She's upstairs in her room. I was just fixing a dinner
tray for her. She still can't put much weight on her bad
ankle and I've insisted she not try to navigate the stairs with

the crutches. Even on a flat surface she has trouble with them, with her sore ribs.''

"I'll be happy to take the tray up to her. I'd like to surprise her.''

A few minutes later he started up the stairs, tray in hand. The door to her room was ajar and she was seated in an armchair between the bed and the window, her foot propped up on a low stool. An open book lay in her lap, but she stared out of the window rather than at the pages. He watched her for a few seconds before pushing the door open.

His action caught her attention and she turned her head to stare open-mouthed toward the doorway. Her lips formed his name, but no sound came out. Her gaze never strayed from his face as he strolled across the room and set the tray on a table beside the chair.

Carefully sliding her foot to one side of the wide stool, he made a space between it and the chair and sat down, facing her. "Hello, Caroline.''

"What—what are you doing here?''

Derek lifted her hand from her lap, turned it over and placed a soft warm kiss in the center of the palm. He raised his head and looked into her eyes.

"I was going to ask you the same question.''

"What do you mean? I live here.''

He nodded. "I guess that's not the right question. What I really wanted to know is why you ran away from Atlanta.''

She tugged gently at her hand, but he held onto it. "I don't know what you mean. I was already overdue to return home.''

"So you felt it necessary to go directly from a hospital bed to catch a flight, alone. I understand that your injuries weren't serious, but you should have taken a few days to recuperate when you left the hospital. You can't give me the excuse that you had to return to work. Obviously, you're not well enough for that.''

Caroline bit her lip. She could think of nothing to say. It had occurred to her that he might eventually call and ask for an explanation of her abrupt departure. She never considered the possibility that he would follow her to Connecticut.

Derek pulled a slip of paper from his jacket pocket. ''The nurses' aide found this in your room after you left. She asked me to see that you received it.''

He held it out to her and watched her open it. She knit her brows in confusion as she read.

*"Sweetheart, I had to leave to take care of a problem at one of our job sites. I don't know how long it will take, but I'll be back later. Love, Derek."*

She shook her head. ''I never saw this before.''

Derek nodded. ''I suspected that when the nurses' aide said she found it under the bed.''

''The nurses' aide?'' she asked, forgetting that he had mentioned that bit of information earlier.

He took both of her hands in his. ''When I got back to the hospital, you were gone and she was making up the bed. I remembered that the doctor said he might discharge you. When I found out you weren't at Ian's, I called Vanessa and she told me you had gone home.''

Caroline shrugged. ''You said you'd stay with me. I thought I remembered seeing you sitting in the chair when I sort of woke up a few times. When I woke up for real yesterday and today, you weren't there. This morning I asked the nurse if there were any visitors waiting to see me. She said there was no one waiting and she didn't mention that you had ever been there. I thought I'd imagined seeing you.''

"How could you think I'd desert you? I love you, Caroline."

Misty-eyed, she caressed his cheek. "I love you, too, Derek."

She blinked back the tears. It was unnecessary to mention her notion that Ian might have been upset about the ransom money.

"Can we just say I wasn't thinking very clearly because of the medication?"

He stood up, lifted her from the chair and sat down in it. Pulling her gently onto his lap, he whispered, "As long as you tell me it was all a mistake, I'll take whatever excuse you want to give me."

He kissed her, tenderly at first. When she entwined her arms around his neck, he deepened the kiss. He pulled her closer, stroking her back.

Caroline caressed the nape of his neck, but that was not enough. Her hands moved to his shoulders and then to his throat.

He tightened his arms around her and she winced. Derek loosened his hold. It was time to call a halt. With some effort, he lifted his head, breaking the kiss. He sighed.

"Your dinner's probably cold by now."

She shrugged. "That's okay. It can always be reheated in the microwave."

Derek grinned. "And what do suggest I tell your mother we were doing to allow your food to get cold?"

Caroline nuzzled his neck, gently tugging at his ear with her teeth. "I don't think she'll ask any questions. She's amazingly perceptive."

Derek chuckled. "And you're going to send me down there to face her speculating looks."

Caroline looked at her injured ankle. "Well, I am an

invalid, remember. I can't be trekking up and down the stairs with my bad ankle.''

He slid her from his and lap and set her on her feet. When he vacated the chair, Caroline moved to sit in it. She gasped when he scooped her up in his arms.

''That's a problem that's easily solved.''

''Derek you can't carry me down the stairs. It's too dangerous.''

''Trust me.'' He started toward the bedroom door. ''I'll come back up for your tray.''

Grace looked up from her task at the kitchen counter when she heard them approaching. Her eyes widened when Derek entered the dining area with Caroline in his arms.

''She decided she'd rather join you for dinner instead of eating alone in her room,'' he explained, glancing in Grace's direction.

He set Caroline down and pulled out a chair for her. After seating her, he placed a brief kiss on her surprised lips. Then he grinned.

''You're really enjoying this, aren't you?'' she whispered.

He chuckled. ''Immensely,'' he murmured, his lips inches from hers. He straightened up and said to Grace. ''I'll get the tray. I'm afraid the food's cold, though.''

''That's no problem. There's plenty here that's still hot. I hope you're planning to join us.''

''Thank you, I was hoping you'd ask.''

Harry had joined his wife in the kitchen when Derek returned a few minutes later. ''Is there anything I can do to help?'' he asked, setting the tray on the kitchen counter.

''No, dear, you just have a seat.''

Derek noticed that she had added two more place settings to the table. He took the seat beside Caroline.

The early part of the dinner conversation was general. Derek asked about their holiday and they told him about their visit to Pittsburgh. Later, when Grace mentioned her daughter's accident, Derek glanced at Caroline. It was obvious that they had accepted the explanation of her having fallen down the stairs.

"When Caroline called and said she was on her way home, Harry and I decided to come and spend some time with her. I knew she'd have trouble managing with her injuries."

Caroline smiled. "I tried to talk them out of it, but you know how mothers are," she said. She took a sip of water and almost choked on it with Derek's next comment.

"If you two would like to get back home, I'll be glad to stay here and look after Caroline. I plan to be in town for at least a week."

Grace suppressed a smile at her daughter's reaction. She turned her attention to her food.

Harry cleared his throat. "That's very kind of you, Derek. As a matter of fact, I have a project that I've been working on. I'd like to finish it before Christmas." He looked at his wife. "If it's okay with you, honey, I guess we can plan to leave in the morning."

Grace nodded. "That'll be fine, dear. I'm sure we'll be leaving Caroline in good hands." She glanced at her daughter.

Her mother's last words raised an embarrassing picture in Caroline's mind. Her mother called her name and she shook off the disturbing image.

"Is that all right with you, dear?"

"Sure, Mom. I can manage, even without Derek."

"Yes, I know. You've been telling me that, but I feel better knowing that you won't have to."

# Chapter Twenty-two

The next morning, Caroline sat in the kitchen with her mother, drinking their second cups of coffee. Derek and her father had taken her parents' bags to the car. When they returned a few minutes later, her mother rose from her seat.

"All set?" Harry asked.

"I'm ready when you are."

They each hugged Caroline in turn and, with the help of her crutches, she followed them to the door. Harry helped Grace on with her coat and opened the door.

"Don't forget your medicine and the ice packs, baby."

Caroline fought the urge to roll her eyes. "I won't, Mom."

Caroline watched them drive away with mixed feelings. Their absence would give her more time alone with Derek. The fact that she was looking forward to their departure aroused some guilt. The idea of being alone with Derek also aroused a few more pleasant emotions, as well as a hunger that she had managed to suppress until that little kiss in her bedroom.

Later, as they relaxed in the living room, she tried to keep her mind off that hunger and the anticipation of having it satisfied. Since her parents had occupied her only other bedroom the previous night, Derek had bedded down on the sofa. At the time she wondered that he had not arranged to stay at a hotel. After his comment to her parents that morning, she understood his reasoning.

The question of where he would sleep tonight ran through her mind. He had carried his luggage upstairs and hung his clothes in the guest bedroom, but if she had her way, he would not be sleeping there. For the moment she was content to lie on the sofa with her head in his lap, her eyes closed.

"How are your ribs? Your mother mentioned the ice packs and medication. Is it still very painful?" Derek asked, stroking her hair.

"It's not too bad."

"Only when some idiot squeezes too hard?" he asked, placing a kiss on her forehead.

"Did you hear me complaining?"

"When do you go back to work?"

"Next week. Speaking of work, how does Ian feel about you taking time off to come here?

Derek grinned. "When I told him you had run away from me again, he was all for it."

Caroline's eyes flew open. "You didn't tell him that?"

Still grinning, he explained, "Not in exactly those words. I told him you had returned to Connecticut."

Late in the afternoon, Derek offered to go out for Chinese food. He returned with an assortment of food, as well as two movie videos.

Caroline followed him to the kitchen on her crutches. When she began taking the dishes from the cabinet, he stopped her.

"I'll do that. You should have that ankle elevated."

"My ankle's a lot better now," she insisted.

Derek walked over to her and pulled up the legs of her slacks. "It still looks swollen to me."

He turned her around and gently pushed her toward the dining area. Earlier that afternoon, he had reminded her of her medicine and brought the ice packs for her ankle and her ribs.

"What did you do, sign a pact with my mother?"

"No, but I told her I'd take good care of you, remember?"

After she was seated at the table with her foot on another chair, he returned to the kitchen. A few minutes later, he had set the table and placed the cartons of food in the center.

"What movies did you rent?"

"One for each of us." He named a recent romantic comedy and a spy thriller.

"Actually, they both sound good."

"Hmm, and I suppose you're going to tell me you like watching sports on television, too?"

"Sometimes."

"That's good to know. I'll remember you said that."


Halfway through the second movie, Caroline started yawning. Her eyelids became heavy. She fought the drowsiness and tried to hide it from Derek. Sitting in the shelter of his arm, her head resting against his shoulder, it would have been so easy to drift off to sleep. With a great deal of effort, she managed to stay awake through the closing credits.

After rewinding the movie, Derek turned off the VCR

and the television. He removed his arm from around her shoulder and glanced over at her.

"I think it's past your bedtime."

"This is why I don't like taking that medication."

Derek stood up and helped her to her feet. "Let's go, sweetheart."

He helped her up the stairs and stopped in the doorway to her bedroom. He took her face in his hands and kissed her lightly.

"Don't look at me like that. Sweetheart, as much as I want to make love to you, I think I'd better sleep in the other room tonight."

Caroline said nothing. The pain in her side told her that he was right. She nodded.

"I'll get fresh sheets for you."

Derek cleared his throat. "Your mother already did that this morning. Do you think that she was giving me a hint?"

Caroline smiled. "Would it matter?"

He chuckled. "Not unless she's hiding in the closet."

Caroline giggled. "I was just picturing that possibility."

He took her in his arms. This time, the kiss was filled with the promise of things to come.

"Good night, baby," he murmured when he raised his head.


Caroline was still asleep the next morning when Derek called Ian. "I thought you might be interested to know that everything is fine once again. The reason for her sudden departure was as I suspected. She blamed it on the fact that the medication made her thinking a little fuzzy. At that point, I didn't care why she misunderstood my absence."

"I'm glad to hear that. Caroline called Zoe soon after

you left. She assured Zoe that her departure had nothing to do with Zoe or the kidnapping. When she didn't mention you or ask about you, Zoe thought it was best not to tell her that you were on your way to Connecticut. I guess she was surprised to see you."

"You could say that. I plan to stay for about a week if you can manage without me. Caroline's still recuperating and there are a few loose ends to be tied up."

"A few loose ends, huh? I won't ask what that means. I think we can manage for a week." Ian chuckled. "Good luck with your loose ends."

"Thanks, I'll call you."

Later that day when they had finished eating lunch, Derek cleared the table. After loading the dishes in the dishwasher, he turned to face Caroline.

"I have to go into Hartford for a while this afternoon. Is there anything you need at the store?"

"No, I don't think so. Do you have another computer job?"

He shook his head. "Not really, just a minor adjustment. I shouldn't be gone more than a couple of hours." He walked over to the table. "Do you still have my cell phone and pager numbers?"

"I think so, in my purse."

He took out a business card and gave it to her. "Both numbers are on there. If you think of anything you need or you run into any problems, call me."

He lifted her to her feet and wrapped his arms around her. "And no running up and down the stairs while I'm gone."

"I'll think about it."

* * *

Derek returned a few hours later to find Caroline asleep on the sofa. After a trip to the kitchen, he returned to the living room. He walked quietly to the sofa and knelt down beside her. She stirred and opened her eyes when he kissed her forehead.

She yawned, sat up and stretched. "Hi, how did it go? Did you finish the job?"

He sat down beside her and turned to face her. "It wasn't really a job. I went to talk to Aaron."

"Aaron? My Aaron? When did you decide to do that?"

He took her hands in his and kissed each knuckle. Then he looked up and met her gaze. His thumbs continued to caress the knuckles that still tingled from his kisses.

"I made that decision while you were in the hospital. I called from Atlanta and spoke to his mother."

"What did she say?"

He smiled. "Well, she wanted a lot of information about my credentials. When I mentioned your name, it opened the door."

Caroline nodded.

"I thought a lot about what you said, even before the kidnapping. Afterward, I remembered how determined you were to save Aaron from himself before he got into something he couldn't get out of. My own words came back to haunt me."

Caroline knit her brows. "What words?"

"My pronouncement that maybe he deserved to be punished if he was a hacker." He shook his head. "The kidnapping made me realize that what he was doing was minor compared to other crimes. Although his crimes are a far cry from kidnapping, I decided that your suggestion might be an opportunity to keep him from getting into more dangerous territory. I came to the conclusion that a request for me to have a talk with the young man about the error of his ways was a small favor to ask from the woman I love."

"So you went to see him. What happened?"

"At first, he wouldn't admit to anything. When I told him I knew he had tried to break into the insurance company's system, I think it scared him."

"You traced him?"

Derek shook his head. "No, but I needed an edge to get him to talk to me. Besides, I think it's only a matter of time before he would be caught. He's good, but he's young and he's not that good yet."

"He admitted it, then?"

Derek shook his head. "Not exactly. I hit a nerve with the insurance company, though. He went off on a tirade about the unfairness of the insurance companies. He insisted they deserved a few problems because of what they did to their clients. When he stopped raving, his mother explained the real source of his anger."

"His mother knew what he was doing?"

"No, I don't think so. Everything fell into place for her when I mentioned the insurance company. Until then, she had no idea he had overheard a conversation she had with his father during one of his visits."

Caroline remembered that Aaron's parents were separated. "I don't understand."

"He has a terminal illness—the father, that is. The insurance company has refused to pay for a treatment that they consider experimental."

Caroline frowned, shaking her head. "What could Aaron hope to accomplish by breaking into the insurance company's system? Was it just revenge for their refusal to allow the treatment?"

"No, he was looking for more than revenge. His plan

was to get into the system and try to change the policy terms. If he changed it in the computer system, when the hospital called to check the policy, the system would show that the treatment was covered.''

Derek sighed. ''His reasoning was that even if the hospital was later denied payment, it would be too late. His father would have received the treatment he needed and it would be put down to a computer error.''

Caroline shook her head. ''So now what will happen to his father?''

Derek shrugged. ''I don't know.'' He looked down at the hands he still held in his.

''Derek, is there something you're not telling me?''

He looked up at her and shrugged. ''Not really. I simply suggested that there might another source for the funds his father needs for his treatment. I also suggested Aaron should consider putting his talents to a more constructive purpose.''

She nodded. ''I see.''

''Caroline, I really don't know if there's anything more I can do to help his father. I don't even know what the treatments will cost.''

She leaned toward him and kissed his cheek. ''It doesn't matter. The fact that you're trying to help is all that's important.''

He loosed his hold on her hands. ''I almost forgot.'' He stood up and started toward the kitchen. ''Wait here.''

He returned a few minutes later with an enormous vase of flowers. The bouquet contained a profusion of roses, lilies, spider mums, and other blossoms.

Caroline stared open-mouthed as he approached. ''I don't know what to say,'' she murmured as he set the vase on the coffee table. She leaned forward, inhaling the fragrance.

Derek sat down next to her. He pulled her close to his side and kissed her temple.

"It occurred to me that I had been remiss when you were in the hospital."

Caroline smiled. "I was only in the hospital for two days." She kissed his cheek. "Thank you, for everything."

Later that night, Caroline's frustration showed on her face when Derek kissed her good night at her bedroom door. She bit back the words that were on the tip of her tongue. It was true, she still had some pain around her rib cage, but this was getting ridiculous.

Derek hid his own frustration. He wanted her badly, but he knew it would be more frustrating if he started making love to her only to realize that she was still in a great deal of pain.

The next morning, Derek was standing in the hallway when Caroline exited the bathroom clad only in a towel. His gaze slowly traveled down from the still-moist skin of her shoulders to her bare feet. He grinned.

"Good morning," he murmured, leaning down to kiss her cheek.

"Good morning. The bathroom's all yours."

When the bathroom door closed behind him, she entered her bedroom. After donning her robe, she went downstairs and started the coffee. She opened the refrigerator with the idea of preparing breakfast, but closed it again. A plan formed in her mind and she grinned.

Walking as fast as her bad ankle would allow, she made her way back up the stairs. Rather than going to her own bedroom, she made a detour to the guest room. She found what she was seeking easily and hurried across the hall to prepare for her surprise.

Derek exited the bathroom shortly after Caroline returned to her bedroom. Her door was closed, but he detected the aroma of coffee brewing. He turned toward the guest room, but veered when she called his name.

"Could you come here for a minute, please?"

He pushed open her bedroom door. The muscles in his abdomen tightened in response to the sight that greeted him.

Caroline was seated in the middle of the turned-down bed, totally nude, with her arms spread along the top of the headboard. Her legs were stretched out in front of her, crossed demurely at the ankles.

"I decided that my ribs are sufficiently healed. The ache from the ribs is secondary to this more pressing ache that can't be eased by ice and pills. You were so concerned about my well-being, I thought I should let you know."

Derek approached the bed with a wide grin on his face. He reached the side of the bed and, with the flick of a finger, sent the towel at his waist tumbling to the floor. "I think I'm beginning to appreciate that wanton streak more and more each day."

"You did promise my mother you'd take good care of me and you've been terribly remiss in your duties."

He chuckled. "I don't think this is what your mother had in mind."

Caroline cocked her head to one side. "Oh, I don't know. She did say she felt confident that she was leaving me in good hands."

"Hmm, now that you mention it, I do recall those words. It does sort of leave her meaning open to interpretation."

He sat down on the side of the bed and began stroking her legs, slowly working his way up from her ankles. When his hand reached the soft pelt at the top of her thighs, he leaned forward and captured one breast with his mouth. He had been starving for the taste of her and now he feasted hungrily. He knew he would never get enough of her.

Caroline removed one hand from the headboard and clasped the back of his head. Her breathing difficulty had nothing to do with injured ribs. Her legs parted automatically when his fingers probed the moist, sensitive area hidden by the silky triangle of hair.

Derek's lips left her breast and he started to rise from the bed, but she stopped him. "I'm not quite prepared for this, baby," he insisted.

Caroline removed her hand from the back of his head and pulled open the drawer of the nightstand. "I think you'll find what you need in there."

Derek chuckled and lifted the foil package from the drawer. "I see you believe in being prepared."

"I took it from your room a few minutes ago. I didn't want you to have to interrupt the proceedings."

A moment later, his hand resumed its explorations. His mouth returned to its previous occupation and Caroline sighed in contentment.

Derek eased closer to the center of the bed and slid his other hand behind her, pulling her closer to him. He questioned the wisdom of that move when she reached down and stroked the mat of hair surrounding his shaft. Derek moaned when her hand closed around the shaft itself. He parted her legs widely enough to ease one across his thighs. Seconds later, she was straddling those thighs.

"I think it's time to take care of that other ache," he whispered. His hands clasped her derriere. They moaned in unison when he entered her.

Caroline crossed her legs behind him as he guided her into the rhythm of his thrusts. She breathed in his intoxicating scent as her tongue traced a path up his neck, then to his chin, and finally met his parted lips. They each tasted hungrily of all the other offered until they could hardly breathe.

Derek broke the kiss and turned his attention, and his lips, to her breasts, laving and suckling each one in turn. Then he leaned back slightly and with one final thrust, brought them to the heights they had been seeking.

Caroline collapsed against his chest, the beat of his heart pounding in her ear. Her hands stroked his back, her own pain forgotten.

Derek eased her from his lap and onto the bed. They lay there crosswise on the bed, locked in each other's arms for a while longer.

When he leaned up on his elbow, Caroline moved to sit up. Derek restrained her. "This might be a good time for a question I've been considering for some time."

His hand caressed her thigh. "How do you feel about moving to Atlanta?"

Caroline smiled. "I think I'd like that. There's just one problem. I'm not sure how easily I could find a job there."

"Baby, you missed the point. I know you probably want to continue teaching and eventually, I'm sure you'll find a job. That's not really a priority, though. I'm quite capable of supporting my wife."

Caroline's eyes widened. "Your wife?"

Derek grinned. "I'm asking you to marry me. I blew it once before. I have no intention of letting you get away from me again." He kissed her tenderly.

"So, what's your answer?" he prompted.

"I have no intention of making the same mistake twice, either," she assured him, caressing his bottom lip with her thumb. "Yes, Derek, yes, I'll marry you."

He kissed her again. "In that case, I suppose we'd better get up from here. We have a wedding to plan."

Dear Readers,

After reading FALSE IMPRESSIONS, many of you wrote that you wanted to hear more about Derek. As I considered that possibility, I decided that I would go one step further and include Caroline, Jason's sister, from STEP BY STEP.

I also decided to add a little danger, as I did in FALSE IMPRESSIONS. As in all of my stories though, the basic message deals with the relationship. After all, that's what romance is all about.

I had fun revisiting both families from the other two novels. I hope you did, too, and I hope you enjoyed Derek and Caroline's story.

Marilyn Tyner
P.O. Box 219
Yardley, PA 19067-1312
mtyner1@juno.com